WANT TWO FREE EBOOKS?

Visit **nikikeith.com** to read *The Perfect Ride* and *The Perfect Daughter*.

CRUSH

NIKI KEITH

Crush

Copyright © 2022 by Niki Keith

For my little-big bro. Thanks for always believing in me.

1

PHOEBE

Fischer (everyone called her Miss G) kept checking in on me as if I were on the brink of a breakdown. No offense, but all I knew about Coach Thorne was that she was a middle-aged, high-strung volleyball fanatic who despised me.

"I can tell you don't eat, sleep, and breathe volleyball," she used to say, scowling like she smelled shit on me. At least her intuition wasn't far off. I sucked at volleyball, but since Laura and Mimi were on the team, I *had* to get involved.

Sighing and pressing my hands together, I sat in Miss G's office, patiently awaiting her return—and by patiently, I mean counting the seconds until the oil diffuser on her desk shifted colors and released its lemon fragrance. Seventeen... Eighteen...

"I'm so sorry about that," Miss G announced as she burst into the room with an exasperated sigh. "Principal McGee can be such a scatterbrain." Rolling her eyes while closing the door, she added, "Okay, where were we?" She paused briefly to smooth her hands over the white pencil skirt paired with a red and white striped mock-neck top, exuding a classy, sophisticated allure.

I really admired Miss G. Since starting at Richmond High a month ago, she had become my confidante—not only as the guidance counselor and cheerleading coach but also as someone more approachable than any therapist I had ever met. Always down-to-earth, she greeted me with a warm smile regardless of the circumstances. With her curly blond bob framing her heart-shaped face, she reminded me of a young Charlize Theron.

She clapped her hands, her eyes suddenly beaming. "I remember." She hurried behind her desk, heels clicking on the wooden floor. After rummaging through a drawer, she pulled out a teal fur-covered journal along with a matching pom-pom pen. "Ta-da," she declared, holding out the items.

I squinted in confusion. "A *gift*? I thought you wanted to discuss Coach Thorne."

Miss G nodded. "We'll get to that. First, I want to congratulate *you* on all your accomplishments. So, take this." She shoved the book towards me.

I accepted it with a shaky hand, admiring the teal cover—my favorite color. "It's beautiful."

"Good!" Miss G chirped as she settled into her chair. "The idea is for you to document your journey. You've achieved so much in the past few weeks. You've gotten those grades up, made the volleyball team, joined the cheerleading squad." She did a little dance, making me smile. "And now, you're off your medications. There's just no stopping you, Phoebe. I love it!" Her blue eyes sparkled as she studied my face.

But damn, the way she put it made me sound like some driven overachiever, which was hardly the case. Sure, I'd accomplished plenty, but whenever I reflected on my life *before*, I couldn't help feeling embarrassed.

Miss G smiled sympathetically. "How do you feel about everything?" she asked, practically reading my thoughts.

I shrugged, nibbling on my bottom lip and forcing my breaths to stay calm. As I gathered my thoughts, I stared out the small window behind Miss G at the trees rustling in the breeze. I always had to choose my words carefully when talking to Dr. Landry—after all, diagnosing me on a whim was his special power—but with Miss G, I didn't have to pretend.

Then she leaned in closer, catching my gaze.

I lowered my eyes to my lap. "I'm still ashamed of my past. I mean, I *thought* he was real, you know. Every turn I took, I saw him—alive and well—and that feeling was so irresistible that I just wanted to hold onto it tight." I peeked at Miss G and caught her troubled expression. Forcing a laugh, I straightened my posture. "But, of course, I know it was only a figment of my imagination. That shit is done." I waved my hand, trying to appear nonchalant. But like I said, that was Miss G. And though she was cool and all, she still read me like an opened book.

She reached across the desk and squeezed my shoulder. "It's hard to say goodbye—I get it. Losing someone you love is one of the most tragic things we can experience. But remember, we all process loss differently, Phoebe.

There's nothing to be ashamed of. Everyone who cares about you isn't insisting you simply move on; we just want you to push ahead and embrace all the great things life has in store. That's the purpose of this journal: to document your journey as you reclaim control over your life while keeping your father's loving memory right here." She placed a hand over her heart. "No one can ever erase him from you."

I brushed my fingers across the soft journal and flipped through the blank pages, a surge of excitement pulsing through me at the thought of filling them with words. *My story.*

"Do you think you're ready to forgive your mom?" Miss G asked suddenly, toying with the pens in the cupholder.

I scowled—*fuck no*—on the tip of my tongue. "I wouldn't say I've come *that* far."

"You shouldn't hold a grudge against her forever. Acceptance is part of moving on, too, you know."

Like hell it is. I rolled my eyes as Miss G tucked her hair behind her ear, and the sparkling diamond on her finger caught my eye.

I gasped. "Is that what I think it is?"

She pulled back slightly, staring at her ring as if for the first time, her cheeks going red. "Yes. My fiancé, Chuck, finally popped the question. We're getting married next spring."

"Congratulations, Miss G! Chuck is one lucky dude."

She tilted her head. "No, it's the other way around—Chuck is super amazing. But while we're on that subject, will you include a journal entry about love?" She rested her chin on both hands and batted her lashes at me.

Love? Please. Dating was the furthest thing on my mind right now. But playing along, I grinned at Miss G devilishly. "We'll just have to see, won't we?"

She waved her finger at me. "Okay. Kiss and don't tell, I suppose." Her giggle, bright and giddy like that of a schoolgirl, made me smile.

"Well, I tell you what," she said, reaching across the desk to grab my wrists. Her thumbs gently grazed my raised scars. "These remind you that your life isn't over. You're a fighter, Phoebe. And whenever you're feeling weak or vulnerable, just look at them and remember you survived because you have a purpose on this earth. I'm a hundred percent sure your father would be so proud of you."

I blinked rapidly as I examined the tattoos on my wrists—my go at masking my suicide attempt. On my right wrist, LOVE was inked, and on my left, LIFE. Dad had taught me patience and the strength to overcome obstacles, always saying there's light at the end of the tunnel. And yet, I had slit my wrists. I felt like I'd disappointed him. I knew Miss G was only trying to help, but her words painfully reminded me of how much I'd fucked up.

I slowly freed my wrists from her grasp. "I better get going," I said, trying to keep my voice light while getting to my feet.

But Miss G rolled back in her seat and stood, too, studying me intently. "Was there something else on your mind?"

"Nope." I turned quickly, clutching the journal to my chest, and started for the door when Miss G stopped me again.

"Okay, and about Coach Thorne?"

I considered that a beat. "All good," I said, glancing over my shoulder. It sounded awful, but it was the truth. I was sorry she passed away, yet my thoughts of Coach Thorne ended there.

Miss G's eyes fixed on me. Satisfied, she lowered back into her chair and rifled through her papers. "Okay. Same time tomorrow," she said, as she always did when our sessions wrapped up.

"You bet." I opened the door to leave and immediately bumped into a guy. He raised a fist as if to knock, then staggered back with his black-framed glasses askew on his face.

"Oh, my gosh. I'm sorry," I blurted. "Are you hurt?" Snuggling the journal beneath my arm, I placed a hand on his shoulder. He was Black, around my age, sporting a thick, curly faded mohawk.

"I'm okay," he said, rubbing his temple while straightening his glasses and casting a disapproving look my way. "Is that the principal's office?"

"No, it's upstairs. I can show you if you like."

He peered at me with the largest brown eyes I'd ever seen. When he fell silent, I offered a smile. A few seconds passed before I cleared my throat nervously, shifting the journal to my other arm.

As if struck by lightning, he jerked and blinked at me. "Sure. Of course." Forced laughter followed. "You must think I'm a complete idiot."

I returned his smile. "Come on." I lead the way to the staircase. "Are you new here?" His cheeks flushed as he bobbed his head. I stuck out my hand. "So am I. I'm Phoebe, by the way."

His grip was warm and gentle. "Ethan."

Once we reached the landing, I turned to him. "Are you in trouble, Ethan?"

He burst into laughter. "What makes you say that?"

"I don't know. You're headed to see the principal."

He craned his neck to look me in the eye. "No. I'm not in any trouble."

I waited for him to elaborate, but we walked in silence the rest of the way. "Here we are," I announced as we stopped outside the office door.

"So soon?"

"No worries. I'm sure you'll get lost again."

He bit his bottom lip as he considered the idea, eyebrow raised. "What's your number? You know, just in case I do get lost."

I clicked my tongue. "Pretty smooth."

"What?" he replied in mock innocence. Before either of us could add anything more, Principal McGee swung the door wide and ushered Ethan inside.

I stuck my tongue out at him just as the door closed. Laughing, I hurried back to the staircase, thinking about how Laura and Mimi must be losing their minds over my absence. Just as I suspected, Laura and Cassie—both part of the cheer team—were waiting by the lockers.

We shared visual arts class together. They'd enrolled for extra credit, but art was my passion—sketching, painting, photo editing, you name it. I was completely devoted.

"Why'd that bitch keep you so long?" Laura Preston demanded.

Frowning, it took me a moment to realize she meant Miss G.

"Bitch? I thought Miss G was cool, right?" I glanced at Cassie for backup. Cassie Lang was our flyer, unquestionably the cheerleading squad's star: blond, short, and petite, making her an easy pick for lifts and tosses. Her sea-green eyes were locked onto Laura, silently awaiting judgment. When neither girl responded, I shook my head. "Anyway, where's Mimi?" Normally, she clung to Laura's side. But I spotted her in a corner, talking with...

I squinted to be sure. "What's Mimi doing with *Mr.*

Diggs?"

Cassie gasped beside me, noticing them, too.

Mr. Diggs, the creepy janitor, was rumored to lurk in the girl's bathroom, spying on us. Geoff Diggs, nearly fifty, was scrawny and only about an inch shorter than me. The kids called him Mr. Greasy due to a constant sweating condition that left his grey jumpsuit permanently stained. From beneath his bed of dirty, dark strands, his beady eyes scanned every detail of Mimi.

I shuddered while turning away, my insides quivering. "I'd be sick if he looked at me like that."

"Well, he does, Phoebe," Laura said. "Don't you know he has a crush on every new girl?"

"What?" I sputtered, my eyes widening.

Cassie nodded. "Yep. It used to be me before you came along. Thank God."

I swallowed. "How do you know when Mr. Diggs has a crush? What exactly does he do?" Laura and Cassie snuck each other glances, and I was left hanging. "Come on, guys. What the hell?" My heart pounded ten beats per second. Mr. Diggs was such a creep.

In a low, almost sinister tone, Laura replied, "He sidles up behind you and whispers about how he'd like to tie you up in his cellar. Oooh." Cassie chimed in, both of them playfully flicking their fingers at me.

Giggling, I swatted them away. "Y'all are so lame."

"Alright, seriously, what did Miss G want?" Laura asked, folding her arms. Cassie stared at me expectantly.

My mouth opened, but I struggled to find words. I wasn't ready to tell them about my sessions with Miss G. They knew nothing about my past either, so they really wouldn't get it. "We—she wanted to know how I was doing because of the Coach Thorne thing."

Laura scoffed and tossed her dark curls over one shoulder. "Coach Thorne-in-Our-Ass? So, *what* it was her time to go. We all have to someday. I can't believe she kept you to talk about her."

"Who kept what, what?" Mimi interjected as she approached, dressed in a short, pleated, peach-colored dress. Mimi—short for Mila—Sanchez sported long, flowing, ombre brown hair. Everyone said she was the spitting image of Ariana Grande; she even wore her hair pulled back in Ariana's signature ponytail. Pointing a glittery nail at Laura, she snapped, "Who are you disgusted with now?"

"Miss G-string," Laura retorted with an eye roll.

"Laura!" My jaw hit the floor. Cassie clamped a hand over her mouth.

Smirking, Laura shifted her weight and tilted her head at us. "Stop pretending you can't tell she's a slut."

"You're just jealous because her tits are bigger than yours," Mimi teased.

Laura cupped her hands beneath her boobs. "At least mine are real." Then her dark eyes flashed. "What do you wanna bet that Principal McGee paid for Miss G's? They've had way too many 'unnecessary meetings,' if you ask me."

"But we didn't ask you, Laura," I said, my tone laced with venom. I couldn't grasp why she'd suddenly turned on Miss G like that.

Each girl turned to me with curiosity gleaming in their eyes. "What?" I cried.

"I didn't know you had a thing for Miss Thang," Mimi crowed as she playfully shoved me. "Welcome to the lesbian club."

"It isn't like that at all," I protested, heading to my locker to stow away my journal. "Miss G is happily engaged. So, I just think you're wrong about Principal McGee."

Mimi turned on Laura, cackling. "Ha! She told you."

Laura, a smile frozen on her face, kept silent. But after a beat, she reached into her palazzo pants and produced a diamond-clustered brooch in the shape of a B. Holding it out to me, she said, "Congratulations. You're officially a Pink Lady."

I stared at the brooch, and then at Laura. "You're joking—right? *Right?*" My excitement meter exploded as Laura leaned in and pinned the brooch on my collar. I flailed my hands, squealing like an idiot. The Pink Lady Club was such a big deal I couldn't even be pissed my brooch simply bore a letter B. Miss G supervised the club, but Laura was the president and diamonds were her latest trend.

The PLC was a tight-knit circle of girls—those ultimate overachievers enrolled in advanced classes, volunteering in the community, and excelling both socially and athletically. They were the smartest, most respected students in school. It'd barely been a month for me at Richmond High, and *I* made the club. As I tentatively ran my fingers over the brooch, Miss G's words resurfaced. Maybe Dad *would* be proud if he could see all I had accomplished.

Mimi looped a slender arm around my neck. "Congratulations, girl."

"Thank you, guys, really."

"How come I don't have *my* brooch yet?" Cassie asked, pivoting toward Laura.

Laura glared at her impatiently. "Haven't I told you already?" Cassie nodded. "And *what* did I say?"

Cassie absentmindedly twirled a strand of hair around her finger. "That my brooch is in the jewelry shop having more diamonds set in it," she replied in a monotone.

Laura craned her neck toward Cassie. "Do you want your brooch to look like a knock-off?" Cassie pouted and shook her head. "Well, then *knock* it off and congratulate Phoebe like the Pink Lady you are."

With a crooked smile, Cassie shot me a quick look, her cheek reddening with embarrassment as she bit the inside of it. "Welcome, Phoebe."

I pulled her into a hug, inhaling her floral-scented hair. "I'm glad to be with you guys."

"Good. Everyone's happy," Laura said, flashing her pearly whites at me just as the bell rang for third period. "We have important shit to discuss at lunch, so be on time." She tapped her wrist.

Before class began, Principal McGee entered. He was a tall, six-foot Black man, solidly built. Rumor had it he once played pro football twenty years ago, yet he didn't look a day over thirty.

"As you all know, we recently lost Coach Janice Thorne. It's been confirmed that she suffered an aneurysm."

Surprised gasps rippled through the room. Somebody started a rumor that Coach Thorne had died from steroids, but I never believed that. Considering my last encounter with Coach Thorne—her screaming at me at the top of her lungs, what a back-row did—a brain aneurysm made sense although it sounded like a painful way to go.

"The news of her funeral is posted on the bulletin board, and we will hold a candlelight vigil tonight," Principal McGee continued, mentioning something about grief counseling when someone interrupted him.

"What's going to happen to the volleyball team?"

"That's a good question," Principal McGee acknowledged, glancing over his shoulder as he signaled for someone to step forward.

In that moment, the most stunning creature I had ever

seen entered the room. I craned my neck for a better look. His shoulder-length dreadlocks were pulled back into a ponytail; vibrant tattoos decorated both of his brown arms. Lean and muscular in all the right places, he casually scratched the stubble on his handsome, broad face, his brown eyes taking in everyone slowly.

"Class, welcome Mr. Little, your Visual Arts teacher—and new volleyball coach."

Laura whistled behind me, prompting giggles from the rest of the group.

"Please, call me Liam," he said smoothly.

"No, no," Principal McGee interjected. "At Richmond we respect our authoritative positions. I better not hear first-name bases," he warned, wagging his finger.

Liam shrugged and slipped his hands into the pockets of his tight-fitting jeans. Damn, he was too sexy. We were so busy gawking at Liam that we didn't notice the younger guy trailing just behind him. He adjusted his backpack, catching my eye—it was Ethan, the guy I had escorted to Principal McGee's office.

We exchanged a brief look before he shyly diverted his gaze.

"Oh—this is my nephew, Ethan," Liam said, draping

an arm around him. Ethan offered a tiny wave, his gaze stuck to the floor.

"Ethan is your new classmate," Principal McGee offered. "I expect you all to welcome him and introduce yourselves when you get the chance." He then motioned toward Ethan, who awkwardly made his way to a front-row seat, his backpack slipping quietly to the floor.

Looking back at Liam, Principal McGee added, "I'll leave you in charge of the room now," shaking Liam's hand and giving him a friendly pat on the shoulder before heading out the door.

Liam waited until the door closed, then turned to us. "Inside this room, I'm Liam. Out there, I'm Mr. Little. Any questions?" He scanned the room.

Are you *single*?

Laura raised her hand. "I want to know—how many tattoos do you have?"

"Uh..." Liam began, "I believe math class is on the second floor," which sent the room into laughter. When he winked at Laura, I nearly melted. Richmond High had just become way more interesting.

2

pHoeBe

EXCITED VOICES FILLED THE CAFETERIA AT LUNCH. Yet at the cheerleader's table, we discussed only one topic *Liam*. It was all we could think about—how incredibly hot he was. Funny. Cool. Easy-going. He even learned our names for the rest of the class and took the time to learn about our goals and dreams.

Laura squirmed in her seat, unable to sit still. "The list of things I'd love to do to that man is endless. Whew!" she declared, fanning herself with her hand.

"*Right*." I agreed, nudging her with my elbow. Across from us sat Cassie and Mimi.

Cassie giggled. "But you've said the key thing," she remarked with air quotes, "*that man*. Legally, nothing can happen between you two."

Laura pointed a stalk of celery at her. "Miss Goody-Two-Shoes and her legal talk—a girl can dream, you know," she replied with an eye roll.

Cassie's cheeks reddened. It was no secret that she dreamed of becoming a lawyer.

Mimi scoffed. "I'm so tired of talking about Liam. He's not even that cute."

Laura shot her a look as if she were from another planet. "Bitch, who are you kidding? He's identical to Lenny Kravitz."

"I rest my case—*not* sexy," Mimi countered.

"Anyway," Laura said, eyes lighting up, "guess who's spending the summer in Rome, Italy?"

"OMG. *You?*" Cassie cried, excitedly grabbing Laura's arm.

Laura rolled her eyes. "No—Santa Claus. Of course, *moi.*"

"Whoa, Laura, that's amazing," I said. "What's the occasion?"

"Well," she began flirtatiously, batting her lashes, "my daddy's taking me to check out colleges."

Mimi quickly interjected, "So, you're really going to

do it—study abroad?"

Laura shrugged. "We're not sure yet. But while I'm away, Mimi's in charge." She glanced at me and added, "I know school's out, but the Pink Ladies are still active. We have to uphold our reputation." I nodded, not quite sure why she was speaking directly to me. "Speaking of," Laura continued, "tonight we're having a PLC meeting at my place to discuss our volunteer routes for next week. I thought we could turn it into a slumber party—show up in your pajamas?" she surveyed the table.

Cassie laughed. "You want us to *drive* there in pajamas?"

Laura huffed, a tight smile on her lips. "What's so funny, Cassie? If I said it, why would you think it's a joke?"

I thought the idea was silly too, but hardly worth sacrificing my brooch. Judging by the daggers Laura was shooting at Cassie, she was on the verge of being kicked out of the club.

"What time, Laura?" I asked, bumping shoulders with her to shield Cassie, but Laura kept her disgusted gaze on her.

"Eight o'clock. And don't even think about bringing that whiny brother of yours like last time. Your mother needs to quit being cheap and hire a babysitter."

Mimi clamped her hand over her mouth, her shoulders bouncing as she whispered, "Her ten-month-old brother kept us up all night, screaming for his momma."

Cassie stuck out her trembling chin defiantly. "I won't let that happen again. So, what's your verdict on the nephew?" she asked, smoothly changing the subject.

My stomach fluttered. Throughout the class, Ethan and I shared secret glances and smiles at one another.

"He's already chosen his pick of the litter," Laura said with a nod in my direction.

I almost spluttered juice over the table. They blinked, waiting for an explanation. After an eye roll, I briefly recounted meeting Ethan earlier.

"Aw," Cassie said, "that's super cute."

Laura groaned. "Lame. The geek doesn't stand a chance. Liam is bae all the way."

"But who *is* that guy? For all we know, he could be a serial—" Mimi stopped in mid-sentence as Rory, my fourteen-year-old brother, and Summer Pankowski landed at our table. *Uninvited.*

Rory sat right beside Mimi, and Summer took the spot

next to him. "What's up?" Rory asked, trying to be chill.

The longer I glared at him, I realized he'd combed back his usually messy dark hair. And that cologne—I couldn't believe it. He was clearly trying to impress my friends. I bit into a carrot stick to suppress a laugh. Rory's confidence was adorable, but he was a junior, and Laura and the others didn't give juniors the time of day.

Laura glared at Rory and Summer. "Can I see your invitation? Oh, that's right—you don't have one because nobody invited you."

Rory blinked at me for help while Summer flashed her bright smile. "I'm here for Phoebe," she said.

"Me too," Rory added.

How lame, I thought, wrinkling my nose at him, but I jumped in to defend them. "It's fine. There's plenty of room, right?"

Laura protested briefly but then relented.

Summer and I shared a smile. Short and chubby with a bubbly personality, Summer kept her short brunette curls in place with a purple headband that perfectly matched her cropped violet cardigan. Apparently, purple was her favorite color. "So," she said eagerly, "we're discussing Mr. Hottie, right?"

Rory puffed out his chest, and I nearly choked on a broccoli floret. "That corny ass teacher? Ew. Come *on*, ladies."

Mimi slapped her palm on the table, excitedly agreeing. "I keep telling you guys, he's *not* all that." Her face fell in disgust.

"We'll just have to agree to disagree, girlfriend," Summer said, reaching over to pat Mimi's hand. "So, Laura—have you chosen the new Pink Lady?"

Oh, *no*. My shoulders slumped instantly. I didn't know Summer wanted to be a Pink Lady, too. I mean, I'd already competed against her during cheerleading tryouts. Summer had skills—she was stealthy and quick on her feet, with perfect toe touches even if she wasn't as strong in stunts and aerials. Still, she could be a great spotter or even perfect for the base, although Laura, our captain, and Mimi, the co-captain, clearly disagreed with my assessment.

Laura grinned broadly. "You're looking at her," she said, nodding in my direction.

Summer blinked slowly at me as her gaze fell on my brooch. Rory flipped me a thumbs-up, but I wasn't in the mood for celebration. I swallowed hard, attempting to force down the lump in my throat while surveying every inch of Summer's face.

"Oh," she murmured softly, her eyes clouding over as they met mine—then her lips spread into the widest smile imaginable. "Congratulations, Phoebe. You deserve it." Her curls bounced as she nodded with over-enthusiasm.

"Summer," I began, my voice low and cracked, though I wasn't sure what to say. I'd already robbed her of the cheerleading position, and now the Pink Ladies? The lump in my throat swelled to the size of a softball.

"I'm sure there'll be other opportunities," Summer said, brightening a bit. "Hey, at least we'll all be on the field together. I joined the school band—I play the tuba."

Mimi rested her elbow on the table and propped her chin in her hand while eying Summer. "Why does that instrument suit you?"

I rolled my eyes. "That's awesome, Summer."

Laura let out an exaggerated yawn. "Yeah, yeah, that's great, Sum. But back to Liam," she said, sparking laughter among us.

"Phoebe, can I see you for a second?" Mrs. Chambers, the English teacher, asked as the last bell rang. She smiled as

I approached her desk, juggling my backpack. Her fuzzy auburn curls were tied up in a messy bun with a pencil stuck through it. Students zipped past, happy as hell they weren't in my shoes.

"I need a slight favor from you," Mrs. Chambers said, tenting her fingers.

"Okay?" I waited for her to go on.

"The new student, Ethan Little?" she asked, motioning toward him. I glanced over my shoulder as he hurriedly stuffed items into his backpack, pretending not to have heard his own name. "I'd like you to be his study partner for a couple of weeks, just to help him catch up with his classes." Leaning in conspiratorially, she added, "He's missed quite a few classes since his transfer."

I nodded. "Sure, Mrs. Chambers. That won't be a problem at all."

"Awesome." With a curt smile, she returned to her work.

I lingered behind to meet Ethan.

He sighed dramatically. "First my tour guide, now my study buddy? You've really got to stop fussing over me like this. I feel too special."

I laughed. "Just your luck, Mrs. Chambers asked *me* to

save your grades."

He eyed me sideways, pushing his glasses up his nose. "You're just as much beauty as brains," he remarked, immediately lowering his gaze.

I tucked my hair behind my ear. "At least now you get my phone number."

His eyes widened as he quickly pulled out his cellphone to exchange numbers. We arranged to meet on weekends for study sessions. Just then, as Ethan and I were chatting a bit more, Zander Bridges appeared and interrupted us.

"Sup, Phoebe," he said coolly in his signature sly tone.

I offered a casual wave and a shrug, though it was hard to remain nonchalant while staring into Zander's magnetic eyes—shifting somewhere between brown, green, and blue. His long, straw-blond hair glinted as if he were in a shampoo commercial. Being blond myself, I felt like we were in a hair competition when we stood side by side.

"So, I heard you're gonna be cheering for me now," Zander said, a pleased grin plastered on his face.

Zander was top of his classes and a standout athlete. As quarterback and captain of the football team—and a pitcher who threw as effortlessly as he dunked—I'd call him the perfect guy, but he was Laura's ex, and therefore *off-limits*.

I managed a polite smile. "It appears so." He gazed into my eyes, as dreamy as ever.

Ethan shifted. "Later, Phoebe," he grumbled, brushing past Zander.

"See you Saturday?" I called after him, but he kept heading toward the doors, pushing them open to leave. What was his problem?

"I guess I better give it a *thousand* percent on the field then," Zander continued.

"Huh?" I squinted, refocusing on the conversation. "Oh, you'll be fine. The Sharks have an excellent record."

Zander flashed his sparkly teeth. "Yeah, you're right. I *do* rock."

Conceited much? I arched an eyebrow. Zander waited as I gathered my things, then walked me to the double doors. Outside, the sun shone like a halo over his golden hair. Licking my lips while smoothing my straight strands over one shoulder, I prepared to leave.

"Do you wanna go out sometime?" Zander came right out and asked. "I know this great Thai place."

I slowly shook my head, the lie slipping out effortlessly. "I'm sort of allergic to peanuts." Although Zander might be perfect, I didn't want to interfere between him and Laura, even if she'd told me a hundred times she was over him. After everything that had happened at my previous school, being part of the Richmond High clique was a blessing—I needed to stay out of trouble.

"Hmm. Okay. Well…" He took my phone from my hand and thumbed on the screen a beat. "There—you have my number. We can figure something out." Handing the phone back, I glanced at the text he'd sent—a winking emoji. "I tried looking you up on social media, but couldn't find you."

"Oh…" My head tilted back. "I don't have any accounts." I once did, but I deleted them when everything went wrong.

"Aren't you full of surprises?" Zander chuckled. "Anyway, I'll text you later, and maybe we can set up a date?"

Uh. *Not.* But I bobbed an agreement to get the conversation over with. When I got to my car, Summer was there waiting, clutching a black instrument case.

"Summer, hey."

Summer gestured toward her case. "Could you give me a lift to the youth center on Edge Street? They offer music classes there, and I need all the practice I can get."

"Sure, hop on in," I said, unlocking the car. "So, the tuba, huh?" I sneaked a look at her once she settled in the passenger seat. "Was that really your instrument of choice?"

She smiled weakly. "Not exactly. They gave me the tuba, so... I'm starting to like it, and plus, playing an instrument will get me extra credits."

"Hey, it's totally worth it."

Summer nodded. "You know the saying—beggars can't be choosers. I'll take anything to prove myself." I knew exactly what she meant, but I kept quiet to hear her out. "You must be so proud," Summer said suddenly. "I mean, if *I* were you, I would be, with all the great things happening to you."

I licked my lips. "It didn't come easily, you know. I'm still struggling in volleyball."

"Yet, you're on the team."

I detected a hint of bitterness in her voice. Had she tried out for volleyball too? Blinking, I focused on the road as I combed my brain for comforting words. "For what it's worth, Sum, I think you would've made an awesome cheerleader. You're beautiful, loud, fun, and spirited. It sucks that there was only one opening, but I'd love the chance to cheer beside you." I glanced at her. "Maybe you and I could practice sometime?"

"Really?"

"Yeah. Just you and me. Our very own power sessions where we can make up cheers for fun."

Summer whipped around, placing a hand on my arm. "Let's get together later!"

I thought about it—if we had a sleepover at Laura's, it might go on all weekend. "Um, I'm not free tonight. PLC is having a meeting, but sometime next Monday would be great."

Summer beamed. *"Perfect,"* she chirped, bobbing her head to her own tune. "Hey, let's follow each other on Insta."

I groaned. Not that again. "I'm not on social media. You can take my number, though." I recited my digits as I pulled the car over in front of the music center. I should've posted my cell number in the newspaper as much as I'd shared it that day. Summer was thrilled, and as soon as I got out, my phone chimed with two texts from her.

"Thanks, Phoebe," she said, grabbing her instrument case as she stepped out. We waved before she disappeared inside.

I clicked through my phone's notifications. Summer had texted—

Chello!

<3

I saved her contact and swiped away her notifications. Just then, my phone chimed again—a text from a number I didn't recognize.

Roses are red, violets are blue

I'm going to kick out your teeth

All thirty-two

3

LAURA

"THAT B BROOCH STANDS FOR BITCH," I YELLED, pressing on the brakes, damn near running a red light.

Mimi screamed from the passenger seat, gripping the dashboard with both hands. "Girl, will you take a chill pill?"

"Zander gave her his number, I know it, Mimi."

"So *what* if he did? You're over, Zander—aren't you?"

When the light finally turned green, I pulled away, clenching the steering wheel. Was I really over Zander? It didn't matter—he was mine, and friends weren't supposed to hook up with their friends' ex. That bitch Phoebe had definitely crossed the line.

Mimi huffed a breath, folding her arms and settling

deeper into her seat. "Obviously, you're not."

"What the hell are you so pissed about it for?" I asked.

Her face scrunched up as though she'd just sunk her teeth into a sour lemon. "I just don't get why you're still holding on to that… good-for-nothing bastard. You deserve so much better than him, and you know it."

I kept my eyes fixed on the road. Sure, Mimi had a point, but she'd never been in a serious relationship. She could never understand how I felt. Zander and I dated for over a year—*captain of the football team and captain of the cheerleading squad*—we were the king and queen of Richmond. Every girl wanted to be like me, and every guy envied him. Like all relationships, we had our issues. We were off and on all the time, but we always made up. Always.

Then Miss Queen Bee entered the picture, and things went off track. But I wasn't ready to let Zander go. Plus, he still had my pictures on social media. That meant something, right? His thing for Phoebe was probably just a bet to get into her pants, and with someone as easy as Phoebe, it wouldn't take long. Afterward, Zander would crawl back to me, finally realizing and appreciating *my* worth. So why waste time getting riled up?

I tossed my hair over my shoulder and gripped the wheel even tighter. "I bet Phoebe thinks she's the ultimate *it* girl. She's such a slut." I glanced over at Mimi, who slowly grinned in agreement.

"She's got nothing on you, girl."

"Hell no, she doesn't. What I can't wrap my head around is what's going on with her and Giselle. Their secret meetings are sketchy, and Miss G was already convinced Phoebe was a Pink Lady as soon as they met. What if they're hooking up too?"

Mimi giggled, playfully shoving me. "Phoebe's a slut, but not a *gay* slut. Miss G—?" She let the idea hang.

Mimi so had a crush on that has-been bitch. I rolled my eyes as I turned onto my street. The closer we cruised to my empty driveway, the further my heart sank. Mom was gone. Again.

"Son of a bitch," I muttered as I zipped into the empty parking space. We got out and began up the gravel path.

"What is it?" Mimi asked.

I unlocked the door and called, "Deena?" My voice echoed in the expanded foyer, hoping the housekeeper was home.

In moments, Deena appeared on the balcony of the

spiraled staircase, clutching a duster. "Yes, Miss Laura?"

"Where's Mom?" I demanded. Mimi and I dropped our backpacks at the door and headed to raid the fridge. Deena scurried down the stairs after us, her brown curls reminding me of a furry rodent. She even *looked* like a rodent, with those beady eyes perched so closely together above a pointed nose.

"Ma'am, the Missus left you a note on the—" she began, but I had already reached the refrigerator and found Mom's stupid note:

Off to the hearing. Will be back later tonight.

Mom

I stared at the words until they blurred together. Mom and Dad's divorce was draining everything away; they'd even argued over who should have custody of me—as if that mattered. Once I turned eighteen, I wanted nothing to do with either of them.

Off to the hearing.

I crumpled the paper and tossed it on the floor.

"Laura, what now?" Mimi touched my shoulder.

I hadn't told her anything about the divorce. Taking a deep breath, I put on my brave face and turned to Mimi and Deena. "Deena, you can take the night off."

She gasped. "But I must…"

I raised a hand to cut her off. "It's fine. Just go. Enjoy your Friday night." She nodded and hurried away before I could change my mind.

Mimi grabbed a carton of Greek yogurt from the fridge. "So, are you gonna tell me what's up?" she asked, peeling back the foil and licking it. Mimi always thought she was *so* sexy.

I handed her a spoon, and we climbed on the stools at the breakfast bar. I whipped out my cell and opened Instagram, thumbs flying over the screen.

"All-night pool party," I typed, "at my place." I then opened my camera. "Lean in," I instructed, pulling Mimi close so our cheeks touched as I snapped a selfie. I loaded it with a shit ton of hashtags and hit post.

Let's see how Mom likes coming home to a bunch of horny kids wrecking her house. I even hoped she'd catch me fooling around in her bed.

"So, no PLC meeting, then?" Mimi asked.

I scrunched my nose. "Those bitches know what they're doing. I don't need to hold their hands." After a quick search for the nearest pizza joint, I placed an order online using Dad's credit card. I hopped off the stool and reached for Mimi's hand. "Come on, let's head to the wine cellar."

"Wait, a second. Phoebe still thinks it's a slumber party tonight—remember, she isn't on social media?"

"Ain't *that* a load of BS?"

"Hell, yeah. Like, who *doesn't* have social media?"

I paused to think. "Maybe someone guilty of sleeping with their best friend's boyfriend." Mimi stared at me. "Seriously, think about it. She moved to a new town and is hiding from social media—she's clearly running from something. I'll bet you a hundred bucks that's what it is."

Mimi burst into laughter. "I have no idea how you come up with this stuff, but are you going to text her about the party or not?"

"*Not*. Let's just let Phoebe show up in her pajamas. It'll be priceless." We both erupted in laughter. "If Phoebe wants everyone gawking after her, then her wish shall come true. *Queen Bee-yotch*!"

4

pHoeBe

"RORY?" I SHOUTED THAT EVENING, AS I STOMPED into the den. He was in front of the fifty-two-inch bouncing and playing a rhythm game on the X Box with the volume at its max. Taffy—my New Yorkshire terrier—trotted over excitedly. I scooped him up in one arm and cupped a hand to my mouth. *"Rory?"*

He glanced over his shoulder, dark brows furrowed—a look that reminded me of Dad—as he swiped quickly at his glistening forehead. "I almost got it."

I grabbed the remote and hit mute. "No, you don't. You can give the *deaf* an earache." Taffy wiggled free and trotted toward the kitchen.

"Ha-ha, hilarious." Rory rolled his dark eyes. "Bet you

won't say that when I'm opening for Red Hot Chili Peppers."

"*Oooh*." I replied, feigning admiration. "An opening act, really? I didn't know video games could harness such talent."

He made a sour face. "Yeah, and just because you can color inside the lines doesn't make you an artist."

That was a low blow. "It's called color therapy," I snapped through clenched teeth. Dr. Landry had suggested adult coloring books to reduce stress, and I've been taking art classes ever since. Oil painting became my specialty.

"Whatever," Rory said. "It's past five. Where have you been?"

"Since when did five o'clock suddenly become my curfew?" I retorted.

He adjusted the collar of his Iron Man tee—two sizes too big—and said, "Well, excuse me for caring." Then he turned and dropped onto the couch.

Sometimes we sounded like an old married couple. My irritation melted away when I saw his saddened eyes. I joined him on the couch with a heavy plop. "I'm sorry. It's been an interesting day," I murmured, thoughts drifting to that creepy poem text.

"So, what? You're Miss Popular again. What's new?" he asked, sinking further into the couch and draping his feet on the coffee table.

"Why put it that way? I'm nothing like the girl I used to be."

"Are you sure?" he shot me a sideways glare. "You're hanging with Laura and the gang like a little puppy."

"Shut up," I said, playfully shoving him. "I'm doing all of that for extra credit and making up for lost time last year during recovery. Cheerleading, volleyball, and the Pink Ladies Club will look a lot better on my college application than '*I had a nervous breakdown in front of the entire school and dropped out.*'" I still cringed every time I said it aloud.

Rory's face fell. He hated it when I mentioned that part of my life—like Mom, he worried I would overexert myself, too delicate on my own. Deep down, I knew they were probably right. I'd been weak when I attempted suicide, hadn't I? I didn't think I was strong enough to go on after Dad died.

Rory had been a soldier, spending every day at my bedside, putting on a brave face and doing his usual annoying kid brother antics to make me laugh. My suicide attempt had left him no room to properly grieve for Dad because he was too busy being there for me.

On impulse, I draped my arm around his thin shoulder.

"What the fudge?" he blurted, frowning as lines creased his forehead. "What the hell was that for?"

I smiled. "Because you're awesome."

He scoffed. "Tell me something I *don't* know." We laughed together.

"Wait—check this out," I said, whipping out my phone. I showed him that text, my *who the hell is this* text beneath it. Of course, I got no response.

Rory mumbled the poem under his breath, a smile slowly spreading. "Somebody wants to kick your ass? Say it isn't so."

I snatched the phone back. "Can you be serious for once?"

He cackled, stamping his feet. "That text scares you? Somebody is just messing with you, Phoebe. You need to relax."

Relax? I frowned. It wasn't as if I felt threatened. Rory was right—it was just a text. But hell, I still wanted to know who it was. I had the right to know. Part of me suspected Ethan. I mean, what was that about earlier? Not only did he ignore me, but when I texted about our study session, he canceled, saying he had other plans for the weekend. He's probably pissed and trying to scare me for whatever reason.

Rory clicked his tongue. "I'm curious about who it is. Because *what* dude is interested in texting you in the first place?"

"Shut up." I laughed, playfully heaving a pillow at him just as my phone buzzed. I pulled it out and frowned.

"Shh, it's Mom." I motioned for him to back off as I answered the third buzz. "What, Mom?"

Mom's voice, warm and caring, followed a few shuffling sounds and a steady beep. "Hi, honey. How are you?"

"I'm fine. How *should* I be?"

"I just heard about Coach Thorne. Why didn't you tell me?"

"Tell you for what?" I cried, running a hand through my hair. "You didn't even know her. *I* didn't know her that well."

She inhaled sharply. "Phoebe, she was your coach. You

had some kind of connection with her. And according to Dr. Landry—"

"I don't *care*," I interrupted. "That wasn't some life-altering event. I'm not going to kill myself!"

Rory shot me a skeptical glance.

"Okay," Mom said, raising her voice an octave. "Well, Rich will be there any minute to check in."

Rich. I cringed. His name was actually Rich—not Richard. Of all places, he'd move us somewhere called *Richmond* Heights. Mom's new boyfriend had once been Dad's best friend—or at least, that's what Dad believed. Rich and Dad had been cops, even partners, but today Rich was a detective.

"I have to pull a double tonight," Mom went on. She was a nurse.

"Rich doesn't need to check up on me, Mom. I'm not a baby."

"*Goo-goo-ga-ga,*" Rory squeaked into the phone. I playfully shoved him aside.

Mom chuckled nervously. "Of course you're not, but he still wants to be there for you. He's cooking dinner tonight—he's even making that strawberry trifle you like."

I glanced at Rory, sticking my finger in my mouth, pretending to throw up. "No, thank you. Besides, I'm going to Laura's in a few hours—we're having a sleepover."

Rory straightened, his eyes narrowing into tight slits. "Without me? I don't think so." He swatted me with a pillow. We had a brief pillow fight while I fumbled with my cell. I held it back to my ear, and Mom's groaning filled the line.

"Phoebe, you can't. I just don't think that's a good idea right now."

"Because Coach Thorne died, I'm not allowed to hang out with my friends? Do you even hear yourself?"

"But Dr. Landry suggests—"

I hung up. I wasn't about to listen to that shit again; I was tired of Mom using Dr. Landry as an excuse to control my life. He'd taken me off my medications because I no longer needed them. But how was I supposed to move on while trapped in her cocoon, cut off from the world?

The phone slipped from my fingertips and landed softly on the plush carpet. I dug my elbows into my knees, leaned forward with eyes closed, and tried to calm down while rubbing my throbbing temples. Mom always made everything worse.

"What are you gonna do?" Rory asked.

Taking a deep breath, I met his gaze. "I'm going to Laura's."

Lips pressed together, he nodded thoughtfully. "Well, in the meantime, I'm gonna nail this tune." He reached over for the remote and restarted the music game. He bounced around maniacally—he couldn't catch the rhythm to save his life—but I cheered him on, laughing and singing along.

Until—

"Hey," Rich called from the doorway. Rory and I both spun around, startled. Leaning casually in the doorframe with his hands in his pockets and a self-assured grin, Rich stepped forward. His forehead was lined with wrinkles; his once-blond hair was fading into grey, and his steel-blue eyes were dull, like a dead fish's. Approaching fifty-something, his slightly bulging belly made me think a button might fly off his shirt at any moment.

"You like it kind of loud, don't you?"

I rose to my feet. Rory and I exchanged furtive glances while he set down the joystick and fidgeted with his loose shirt. I switched off the TV, and it fell into a silence so deep it felt as if the sound had been sucked away.

"You're getting pretty good," Rich observed with an exaggerated smile, baring his nicotine-yellow teeth.

What a liar. Ugh! What did Mom see in him again? Rory said nothing as he continued fussing with his misaligned tee collar.

Rich clapped his hands. "So, I got groceries." He gestured behind him, and I spotted two brown bags overflowing with items in the hall. "I hope you like Italian—Chicken Marsala. My family makes the best marsala sauce." I bent to retrieve my cell; Mom had called twice and texted. Rich forced a laugh at our blank expressions. "You don't seem so excited."

"Yum," Rory deadpanned. "I'll, um, start unpacking the groceries," he offered, backing away from me. I stared at him in disbelief. Was he really going to leave me here with Rich?

"What do you say?" Rich asked, turning his attention to me.

"Um, I'm not that hungry. I'm just going to go to my room and catch up on some homework. Excuse me." I slipped around the couch and passed him quietly.

"Phoebe?" he called. I glanced back. "Diane told me

you shouldn't go to Laura's."

I scoffed. "Of course she did." Folding my arms defiantly, I turned and stomped off to my room.

By a quarter to eight I'd had enough of pacing. After showering and changing into my cozy pajama set—plaid shorts paired with a loose tee—I was ready to go. Laura and Mimi had texted repeatedly, demanding to know where I was, yet Rich was still bustling in the kitchen.

Finally, I grabbed my tote bag and crept down the stairs as quietly as possible. Peeking into the kitchen, I saw Rory setting silverware on the table. He glanced up and pouted when he saw me. I put a finger to my lips and backed toward the front door; Rich was bending near the fridge, so I bolted out.

Richmond Heights sat on the east coast near Florida, where the March heat rivaled summer. The sun had just set, coloring the sky in layers of orange, pink, and purple.

I climbed behind the wheel of my black Fiat 500—its headlights looking like bug eyes—the car Mom and Rich had given me as a bargaining chip after they started dating.

Snickering, I slipped the key into the ignition. "Thanks, Rich."

Mimi awaited me in a two-piece polka dot bikini as I pulled up on Laura's block. But where the hell were her pajamas?

Leaning toward the passenger window with music blasting from Laura's yard, I called, "Hey, what's going on?"

Mimi waved at me excitedly. "Girl, come *on*. Laura's having a pool party."

My jaw dropped. "But I'm in my freaking *pajamas*, Mimi."

She blew a raspberry. "Nobody gives a shit. Hurry up and park!"

I gripped the steering wheel, searching for a spot, but there wasn't one—cars lined both sides of the street, probably because everyone from school was here.

"There," Mimi pointed, indicating a car pulling away from the curb. Sheepishly, I pulled in and felt like an idiot as I climbed out. Mimi rushed over and grabbed my hand, her smirk widening as she took in my pajamas. "Maybe Laura has an extra swimsuit. Let's go," she urged, tugging me around to the back.

I groaned all the way. Laura's backyard was enormous.

Every time I saw it I had the same reaction. "Holy shit," I sputtered, taking in the sight: a blue pool stretching across a football-field-sized yard dotted with palm trees, with dozens of lamp posts casting a hazy, magical glow. As expected, I spotted the entire football team, the cheerleader gang, and several other popular faces dancing, snacking, and splashing in the pool.

"Finally, you made…" Laura approached and paused when her eyes landed on my pajamas. Looking amazing in a black halter top one-piece swimsuit, her dark curls cascaded in two wet ponytails over her shoulders. "Oh," she giggled. "Apparently, we forgot to fill you in on the update."

I glanced down. "Obviously." The word dripped with venom.

She shrugged. "Well, let's just have a good time, shall we?" Grabbing both my hands, she pulled me into a dance. Mimi joined in, and though I wanted to stay mad, the feeling of bouncing and laughing felt too good—I was just happy to be away from home and away from Rich and his stupid marsala sauce, even if I was still in my pajamas.

After nibbling pizza and snacks and dancing a dozen

times, I relaxed in a lawn chair between Cassie on my left and Laura and Mimi sharing a chair on my right.

"Guys—do you recognize that number?" I asked, pulling up the text on my phone. Laura and Mimi read the message and passed the phone between them.

"Somebody's got a secret admirer," Mimi teased.

Laura frowned. "Who wants to send her to the *dentist*? That's disgusting."

"Let me see," Cassie said, reaching for the phone.

Laura gasped dramatically. "It's got to be Diggs."

I groaned, handing the phone to Cassie. "Not that again."

Laura turned to Mimi. "She doesn't believe me about Mr. Diggs. Will you tell her?"

Mimi twirled the ends of her hair. "He's a legit creeper, Phoebe. He even pinched my ass once." Laura frowned. "Okay, maybe it wasn't Mr. Diggs, but *somebody* did. And he was the only person in arm's reach when I *checked*."

"Well, it sure is weird as eff," Cassie remarked, shuddering as she returned my phone. "Could be him."

"Nobody's ever reported Mr. Diggs?" I asked.

"Everyone knows he's a little off..." Laura fluttered her hand. "But people say his family built the school or something, and he's like the last of the Diggs, or whatever. That's why he got a job there—as a janitor," she added with an eye roll.

I shook my head. "Like, where would Diggs even get my number, though?"

"The secretary's office," Laura explained. "She has everyone's info in there, and Diggs cleans her office every day."

That was entirely possible, though I still wasn't buying it. Mr. Diggs didn't seem tech-savvy at all. Besides, he'd never actually done anything to me; in fact, he'd never even spoken to me. There was no way he texted me.

Mimi batted her lashes. "Don't look so blue, Phoebe. It's just a joke. Nobody wants to hurt you."

"Right," Laura chimed in. "We all know you're everyone's favorite."

I frowned. What was that supposed to mean? "Anyway," Laura continued, "if we're going to talk about Richmond High, we might as well mention the sexy parts—like Mr. Visual Arts." She playfully raised her brows.

"Uh-uh," Mimi said, inching toward the edge of her chair. "If you go there, Laura, I'm tossing you in the pool," she threatened, and we all burst into laughter.

A little after one in the morning, I pulled into the garage and snuck into the house as quietly as possible. Laura's party had been awesome—until her mom showed up. Mrs. Preston was a ticking time bomb; she threw everyone out, threatening to call the police and have us all arrested for vandalism, including Laura. It embarrassed Laura in front of the entire school.

Shaking my head, I slipped inside. I never understood parents; it seemed like they were hell-bent on ruining their kids' lives. I entered the warm, dark kitchen where the lingering scent of olive oil and wine from Rich's chicken marsala was unmistakable—it smelled delicious, though probably not as good as Dad's shrimp scampi.

I made my way to the fridge for a bottle of water. The bright light inside cast harsh shadows on the floor. Squinting, I reached in and saw a parfait glass of strawberry trifle sitting on the top shelf with a sticky note that read: PHOEBE

"Aww." My mood softened instantly. I let my tote slip to the floor as I slowly reached in, skimming my finger across the whipped cream and taking a guilty taste. The sweetness settled on my tongue, and I closed my eyes to savor the moment.

"It's not poison, you know," Rich said from behind me.

A tiny yelp escaped as I spun around, eyes wide. There he was at the table with that infuriating grin. Why was he sitting in the dark?

He stepped toward me, hands raised defensively. "I didn't mean to startle you. I waited up for you—your mother's already in bed."

I frowned. "How did you even know I was coming back?"

He shrugged. "Word travels fast. I heard about Laura's big swim party. You didn't get the memo," he said, gesturing at my pajamas with a joking flash of his teeth.

I rolled my eyes. "I take it Mom wanted you to handle this, right?" I turned away to grab a water bottle.

"Diane doesn't know," he continued as I took a sip, and I glared at him. "She thinks you skipped dinner and went to bed early, and I'd like to keep it that way. You came home just past curfew, but..." He waved his hand dismissively. "I'm cool if you are. Cool?"

I hesitated. "Yeah. Cool."

He reached up and squeezed my shoulder. "Okay, let's

get to bed before Diane *really* catches us."

I suppose he expected a laugh, but my lips stayed tight. Disappointment crept over his face, but so what. It hurt to stand there being polite—a smile was a whole other ball game. My stomach knotted up. I grabbed my bag and headed for the hall. "Goodnight, Rich."

He gave a slight nod. "Phoebe?" he called after me. "I hope we can be friends."

I didn't know what to say, so I just nodded and dashed upstairs. Only on the landing did I finally exhale the breath I'd been holding—my chest deflated like a balloon. Rich made me so nervous that I wasn't even sure why anymore.

Tiptoeing toward my room, just past where Mom and Rich slept, I shuddered at the thought of them sharing a bed. If my stomach twisted any further, it might just pop its way out. I fumbled in the dark of my room and shut the door behind me. I was certain I'd left the light on— but maybe Rich had turned it off to strengthen my alibi. Part of me wanted to be grateful, but whatever.

I clicked on my lamp and squealed—Rory was asleep, sprawled across my bed with earphones in and a handheld game pressed against his chest, mouth agape.

Why was everyone lurking around in the dark? Rich, then Rory—was this Scare-The-Shit-Out-Of-Phoebe Day?

"Rory?" I whispered, staggering over and shaking his knee. "Rory?" My voice came out hoarse. He snorted, squinted at me, then let out a loud, panicked wail. "Shhh. Shut the hell up," I hissed. He scrambled upright, his hair sticking out in every direction. "Are you trying to wake the entire neighborhood?"

He yanked off his headphones, looking apologetic. "I'm sorry—I fell asleep."

I folded my arms. "Obviously. But what are you doing in here?" He stretched and yawned sleepily, speaking incoherently.

"English, Rory, not monkey."

He tucked his hands under his armpits and hooted. As badly as I wanted to play tough big sister, I cracked and laughed.

Shaking my head, I crossed to my vanity to brush my hair. "I didn't know you were bilingual." Still in monkey mode, he bounced up on the bed. I spun around. "Okay, knock it off."

He dropped flat on his back again, panting. "I'm in here because…"

Pulling my hair into a braid, I peered at him in the mirror. "Don't tell me—it's that monster in your closet again?" He just stared blankly at the ceiling. "Say something, jackass," I nudged.

His face twisted into a frown. "I didn't want to hear Mom and Rich."

I blinked at him, confused. "Hear Mom and Rich? What are you...?" My eyes bulged. "Oh... disgusting," I moaned between deep gulps of air.

"Tell me about it," Rory said softly, rolling his eyes as he tucked his arms behind his head and stared at the ceiling again. "And you were selfish enough to leave me with them."

"Huh?" I straightened. "Selfish how?"

"You didn't even invite me to the party," he snapped, his dark eyes flashing.

Was I the only one who *didn't* know Laura was having a swim party?

Then his gaze softened. "You know I like them. I wanted to be there, too."

"Rory, to my knowledge, I was going to a *sleepover* tonight. I had no idea about the swim party—if I had, I would have definitely invited you." He scratched his arm and avoided my gaze. Suddenly, I remembered something. I dug around in my tote until I found a lump of aluminum foil. "Look, I even brought you some pizza," I offered as a peace offering.

"Mmm." He stripped it from my hands and bit hungrily into the cold slice.

I frowned. "You're not even going to heat it?"

He blinked. "For what? Pizza is pizza." He shrugged and took an even bigger bite.

I smiled. "Whatever you say."

On Monday, everyone was still talking about Laura's party and her psycho mom. I had thought it would humiliate Laura, but she actually loved every vile comment people had to say about Mrs. Preston. I wasn't exactly in a position to judge, and I didn't defend my own mom either. Still, I felt it was my place to trash her rather than some stranger's.

"How was the PLC meeting?" someone asked as I put away my books. It was Summer. The coldness in her voice hit me like an ice dagger.

I straightened to face her. She wore a flowy lavender top over olive-green leggings. "Summer, hey." I ran a hand through my hair nervously. "That party…" I shook my head. "It was a last-minute sort of thing."

Her eyes dropped as she fidgeted. "Oh. But… even after the fact, you didn't think to invite me?" Before I could reply, she perked up and brushed off her hurt. "No worries—I never get invited to parties."

I shut my locker. "That's not fair. What do you do for fun, anyway?"

"Um, I do lots of things. I enjoy fishing." Instantly, her shoulders slumped. "I know that sounds boring."

I smiled. "It's not. My dad taught me to fish when I was a kid. I'd love to go again."

Her brown eyes lit up. "How about today?"

So soon? I hesitated. "Uh, how about we stick to our previous plans for today and then check our schedules for a fishing trip later?"

"I don't have to—I'm never busy. Anytime is perfect for me," she squealed and bounced on her toes. "I'm super excited. I can't wait to show you where I catch salmon. They literally jump out of the water!"

"No way."

She bobbed her head. "Well, I better get to class now. I'm starting in biology. There's no better way to start your day than cutting up frogs." She chuckled as she headed for the stairs. I raised my eyebrows and forced a laugh. "See you later, Phoebe." She waved and disappeared.

Okay. I slung my bag over my shoulder. *That* was a little weird.

5

pHoeBe

"TWO... FOUR... SIX... EIGHT! WHO DO WE

appreciate?" the cheerleaders shouted, clapped, and stomped. Miss G and Laura sat high in the bleachers, hunched over papers and going through ideas. We had a basketball game coming up against the Wildcats. The half-time show was a cheer-off against the cheerleaders. It was my first dance-off with the squad, and I was hyped.

I shouted with a raw throat, sneakers pounding the floor as I got into it. My legs practically begged to launch into a back-hand spring, but Mimi was being a pain. With Laura and Miss G deep in discussion, Mimi was left in charge, and nothing the squad did seemed to please her.

She paced in front of us, an orange Tootsie Pop in hand and brows knitted into M's, extending a hand like a waitress clutching a tray.

"Louder!" she demanded.

"Goooo Sharks!" we cheered, dropping into synchronized splits as our hands shot up to form a perfect V.

Mimi clicked her tongue. "Your timing was off," she said, pointing at a girl named Shayla. "After two beats, your ass should be on the ground. Can you not count?" Shayla opened her mouth but said nothing, lowering her head as her cheeks reddened.

"You, Phoebe—" she turned on me. "—are leading the rest of the squad. Are you planning on being Team Bee or what?"

A few girls cast skeptical glances my way. "Well, of course not," I sputtered, climbing to my feet. "I'm just excited. This dance-off is going to be a big deal."

"Right," Cassie chimed in. "Aren't there college scouts coming?"

"Who cares about that?" Mimi scoffed, her nose turned up. "We don't need a scholarship. We're trust fund babies."

I wasn't, but I kept quiet. Dad's salary had never been much, and I'd had Christmases with hardly any gifts. Still, Dad always made the holiday as festive as possible with Christmas cookies, hot cocoa, and storytelling beside the fireplace. By my teenage years, they'd promoted Dad.

Rich was always better off than him, which is why we moved to Richmond Heights.

Mimi folded her arms. "Well, there's no I in team, Phoebe," she told me and the girls nodded in agreement.

I placed my hands on my hips, irritated at being put on the spot. "I'm just hyped, Mimi. Calm the hell down." A drop of sweat dripped onto my lash—I blinked it away. "Shouldn't we make the routine a bit more exciting? Like, we're not doing enough stunts." I inhaled deeply, disregarding the piercing look Mimi gave me. I needed to prove that I deserved my spot on the squad. Clasping my hands together, I stomped out a new rhythm.

"S-H-A-R-K! These boys and girls are here to slay!"

I leaped high off the floor, slapping my knees at the peak of the jump. Upon landing, I flowed into a spread eagle, followed by a series of backflips, and finished with a split.

"Goooo Sharks!" I raised my arms in a pointed V.

Some girls gasped in awe as I smiled broadly, chest heaving with pride.

Mimi glared, unimpressed. "Are you done? This is practice, not tryouts."

I slowly brought down my arms, my spirits trampled. That was amazing—and she *knew* it. I got to my feet to protest, but Miss G interrupted.

"Phoebe, you rock," Miss G applauded, looking chic in her checkered yoga pants and grey-and-blue Richmond Sharks tee. She and Laura approached after seeing my routine. To my surprise, Laura wore a grin too. Miss G pointed at me. "That's what we need: more stunts. Laura and I were just reviewing video clips of the Wildcats. They're *flashy*. We have to step it up and dazzle with every move, too."

Mimi slotted back into line with the rest of us cheerleaders, still clutching that stupid lollipop. Laura nodded, her eyes sweeping over us to ensure we understood, but then as Miss G continued, she turned to her abruptly.

"Phoebe, I want you in charge of stunts."

"Huh?" Laura sputtered. "But I always do that."

"Well, yeah," Miss G explained. "But you're better at

creating cheers. And Mimi, you make fantastic dance numbers. We have a dynamic squad—each of you plays an important role."

"True," Laura agreed, flashing me a smile. "That cheer you did was pretty good, too," she told me.

Miss G nodded. "But Laura, you can tighten it up. Add a few extra lines—give it that Laura Love." She bumped shoulders with her.

Laura grinned. "With pleasure."

"Alright then," Miss G clapped, "let's show those Cats what we're made of." We roared back with cheers, our excitement reignited as she led us into the dance routine.

An hour later, I wiped the sweat from my forehead with a drying towel. My stomach and calves ached, but I loved it. I needed that—I hadn't realized how much I missed cheerleading. It'd been three months since a real workout. Back at my old school I'd been co-captain, though I never really cared—our football team never won a game. The Sharks were unstoppable, just like the Wildcats. That match was going to be serious.

"We're looking better, girls," Laura called as we gathered our things. Miss G had already left. A few girls passed, chatting animatedly about the routine.

"Remember, tomorrow we work on partner pyramids, so rest up," Laura added, giving me a tap on the back. "And that solo you did? It was cute—you really know your stuff."

Cute? My eyebrow arched as I forced a laugh. "Miss G thought it was more than cute."

Laura shrugged nonchalantly. "That woman doesn't know everything."

I stared at her smug expression. "Like she said, every one of us plays an important role. No one's trying to take over, Laura." What was *with* her and Mimi? They really had me on the defensive today.

"Oh, I know *that*," she dragged, rolling her eyes. "You don't have what it takes to be a leader."

My breath caught. "Laura, are you *jealous?*"

She stepped back with a high-pitched laugh. "Jealous of you? Jesus, Phoebe, the world doesn't revolve around you. If you want to be part of the squad, you need to get your head out of your ass and learn to be a team player."

I struggled for words. My misstep had clearly upset everyone—several cheerleaders eyed me skeptically, clearly on Laura's side. I couldn't afford more enemies. Biting my trembling lip, I nodded, my voice cracking,

"You're right, Laura. I'm sorry."

Laura sighed and clamped a hand on my shoulder. "Let's just call it a day, alright? On a brighter note, I saw Mr. Handsome peek in during practice." She licked her lips suggestively, trying to get me to laugh. I wanted to, but everything ached—including my face. Laura blinked at me blankly. "Come on, I know you're just quivering inside knowing those sexy eyes caught your sweaty body gyrating."

On the verge of tears, I pretended to dry my whole face with the towel. "I guess so," I murmured into the cloth, muffling my trembling voice. It was hard for me to joke after that blow-up. I couldn't even figure out what I'd done wrong.

Laura said something I couldn't catch. By the time I finished, she was giggling beside Mimi. I shoved my towel and water bottle into my backpack—wishing I could hide my face too—and bolted for the door. As soon as I left, laughter erupted in the gym like clockwork. Climbing the stairs two at a time, I almost collided with Miss G.

"Phoebe—wow, you rocked down there, girl," she said, raising her hand for a high five.

"That's not what everyone else thinks," I stammered,

still shaking.

Her eyes widened. "Are you okay? What happened?"

I shook my head, strands of hair spilling from my ponytail. "Nothing. It's nothing. I'm sorry." I hurried past. Just then, Zander popped up, calling my name. I spun around impatiently.

"Hey, didn't you get my texts?"

"Texts?" I echoed.

"Yeah. I was asking what you were doing after school. Wanna grab a bite to eat?"

"I-I'm sorry, Zander. I'm swamped tonight. Maybe next time," I offered, going, but he caught my arm.

"Wait up. What are you doing later?"

My words choked in my throat. Like, *why* couldn't he take the hint? We were *never* going on a date.

"What is it?" he asked again. "Maybe I can help or just stop by to keep you company." His dreamy eyes pleaded with me.

I had to get away. At any moment, my lunch was going to spur from my lips. "I'll call you later, okay?" I said before dashing through the double doors and stumbling outside. Half jogging, I missed the last few steps; my left calf cramped and gave out. I tumbled off the curb in front of a moving truck, thrashing my arms as I struggled to get up, silently praying the vehicle would stop.

The blue Ford pickup slowed, its shiny chrome grill appearing like silver teeth ready to chomp me down. I pulled myself into an upright position. Aside from dirt and a few scrapes, I was okay.

"What the hell?" the driver exclaimed as his head popped out. It was Liam.

My heart pounded so hard I thought my rib cage might shatter. Could this day get any worse? I wanted to scream.

Liam's eyes widened as he took me in. "Oh my God, are you okay?" The door swung wide and he hopped out, rushing over. "Please tell me I didn't hit you!" He glanced around for witnesses.

"No, I fell," I sputtered, cheeks flushing. I could slap myself. He draped his arm around my waist and helped me to my feet, and I caught a whiff of his cologne— orangey and spicy, perhaps cinnamon.

"Are you hurt? Can you walk?"

I pressed lightly on my left leg; no pain—just tight. "I feel fine."

"Okay, then let me take you home," he insisted.

I almost declined, wanting to manage on my own, but

his strong arm and that spicy scent made my troubles fade. I plopped onto the leather seat. The truck had that new car aroma. He carefully shut the door behind me and went back to retrieve my backpack. Buckling my seatbelt, I couldn't shake the thought of what might have happened—of my mangled, bloodied body beneath that truck. Months ago, I might have broken down at the thought, but now…

Liam reappeared. "All set," he said, climbing behind the wheel and handing me my bag.

I blushed giddily. Quit being immature, Phoebe.

Starting the truck, he asked, "Where to?"

Somewhere far—where we could ride together forever.

"West Seventh Street. It's only a couple of blocks from here." I'll walk to school tomorrow morning and drive my car back.

"West. Seventh. Street," he repeated as he keyed the address into his GPS, apologizing, "Sorry, I'm not familiar with the area yet." His handsome features tensed with concentration as his soft brown eyes followed the directions. "All set," he announced, leaning back and catching my fixed stare.

Was my mouth open? I blinked, scrambling for words, when Liam jumped in.

"How on earth did you fall?"

I shrugged. "My leg just gave out—guess I didn't stretch enough at practice."

He gripped the wheel with one easy hand, completely in control of the truck. "Oh man, you were outstanding—your kicks, your leaps—you looked like a bird in flight."

Wow. This gorgeous creature thought *I* was impressive. Maybe he was just being polite, but I couldn't have cared less. I savored every word.

"Thank you," I managed, feeling sheepish. I sounded *so* lame. Shifting in my seat, I tried to mimic his cool composure, though my eyes roamed over his biceps and my palms turned clammy.

"Are you a gymnast or something? I've always admired Olympic gymnasts. Ethan's a bit of an acrobat too—when he gives a damn, that is." He shot me a playful glance. "Excuse my French."

I smiled. "We're not in a classroom, *Liam.*" His name drifted out sultrily, but he didn't even notice.

"I can't wrap my head around Ethan," he suddenly said. "His sense of humor is odd."

I wanted to ask whether he sent girls threatening texts, but stayed quiet, waiting for Liam to elaborate. The conversation soon fizzled out, and within seconds we pulled up in front of my house.

"Well, I got you back in one piece," he joked.

I laughed a little too hard. "Thank you—I really appreciate it."

"Anytime. You think you'll be alright getting out?" he asked.

As much as I craved the comfort of his arm, I declined. "I should be alright. I can't thank you enough, though." I extended my hand for a quick handshake, just to feel his touch one last time. His gentle grip made me want to close my eyes in awe. When he let go, I gave him my best smile, turned toward the door, and discovered a guitar pick in the cupholder.

"Oh, my gosh—do you play the guitar?" I cried.

He laughed softly. "Yeah—how'd you know?" Leaning forward to see what I was pointing at, he added, "That's my spare. I'm pretty forgetful about little things." He scratched at his stubble. "Do you play?"

"Oh, no." I giggled. "The closest I've come to an instrument is on the X Box." His high-pitched laugh was adorable. "I love the guitar, though."

He grinned. "It's all in the wrist," he said, while strumming an invisible guitar. "My band's called Razor Sharp. It's just a side gig—teaching isn't all that it's souped up to be, you know?"

I laughed. "No shit."

"Hey, we're playing at The Loony Saloon tomorrow night."

My eyes widened. Was he inviting me out?

"Christ," he muttered, slapping his forehead. "What am I thinking? You can't get in."

"Not unless you let me in, like, on a guest list?" I teased.

He narrowed his eyes. "Not a chance." Gently, his palm rested on my shoulder. "See you in class tomorrow?"

I smiled, wishing I could linger in that moment a little longer. "For sure." I grabbed my bag and hopped out, and as soon as I'd shut the door, he drove away. I watched the blue truck turn the corner, feeling a pang of disappointment.

What had I been expecting? Him walking me to the door? A goodnight kiss? It wasn't a date, Phoebe, but it certainly felt like one. In that ride, I'd learned so much about him: he wasn't from Richmond Heights, he loved gymnastics, he thought I was amazing, he played in a band, and he'd be performing tomorrow night. Grinning, I unlocked my front door, already hatching a plan for how to get into The Loony Saloon.

LAURA

"Ow," Mimi whimpered, squirming in her seat. "You're pulling too hard."

"That's because you *won't* sit still," I said, working on the French braids I'd promised her. I hadn't expected my mind to be so full of distractions.

Mimi turned to me. "You still pissed at Miss G for bumping up Phoebe?"

I finished the last braid before plopping beside her on my bed. "I talked to Zander earlier," I admitted—it was our first chat in months.

"*And?*"

I almost laughed at the annoyance in her voice. I so did not give a shit that she hated Zander's guts. But damn, why couldn't I bring myself to hate him, too? How come I still melted every time he looked my way?

"He claims he's seeing someone," I said through

gritted teeth.

Mimi gripped my forearm and gasped. "Phoebe?"

I whipped around to face her. "Who else? That bitch is such a slut—she's stealing everything from me. It's only a matter of time before that bimbo counselor puts her in charge of PLC."

"That won't happen." Mimi tried to offer comfort by smoothing her hand through my curls, but I pulled away.

"How do you know?" I demanded.

She had no answer. "So, what do you want to do?"

"I want Phoebe to burn. I'm so sick of her— I wish I could rip her face off!" I shouted, grabbing a fistful of pillow and squeezing it tightly.

Mimi giggled. "Or you could just knock out her teeth like you mentioned in that text."

I stared at her, eyebrows raised. "I thought *you* sent her that."

"Uh-uh!" She shook her head mischievously. We traded a few silent seconds before I burst into laughter.

"Oh, shit. Who *else* wants to kick Phoebe's ass?"

6

pHoEBe

LIAM, SHIRTLESS AND DRIPPING WITH SWEAT, wrapped up his guitar solo as the Loony Saloon erupted in wild cheers. Laughing, I covered my ears with my hands to muffle the deafening roars while the floor vibrated beneath me. It was utterly exhilarating.

Liam set his guitar aside and strode toward the microphone. "That's a wrap!" he declared with a wave, then leaped off the stage and came over with a smile.

"Come on!" he shouted, grabbing my hand. In hot pursuit, I weaved through the dancing crowd and circled the stage to the dressing room in the back.

He closed the door behind us and pressed his back

against it, his breaths heavy and visible.

"Man, it's so damn loud I can't even hear myself think," he exclaimed.

I laughed and surveyed the cramped room, noting a battered brown sofa, an old clothes rack, and a vanity cluttered with busted bulbs, bottles, makeup brushes, and costume jewelry. The burgundy and beige striped wallpaper was peeling at the edges, exposing water stains beneath.

I felt Liam approach from behind. "I can't believe you made it," he murmured, his warm breath tickling my neck and sending shivers down my spine as he gently spun me around.

My gaze landed on a single droplet of sweat trailing down his chest over his defined abs. I looked up and playfully twirled one of his dreads around my finger. "You owned it up there. I wouldn't have missed that for anything."

"Wow—you look..." he began, stepping back to admire my black miniskirt and white bralette top.

A smile spread across my red lips at his compliment. "I look... what?" I teased, interlacing my fingers behind me. "Tell me." Leaning close, my lips brushed against his

Adam's apple, leaving a bold lipstick kiss with a resounding smack.

He placed his hand gently on my bare back. "You look all grown up. Is that just for me?"

"Only for you, baby," I whispered, licking my tongue along his jawline. His head tilted back as I savored the taste of his neck. He wrapped his arms around my waist, eyes closed, as I sighed into his flesh.

"Oh, Phoebe," he moaned.

Then my teeth sank into his neck, spraying warm blood across my face and staining my white top, and I drank from him with a fierce hunger.

"Phoe-be!" he grunted, my name a distorted cry as gurgles escaped him and he thrashed to break free. "Phoebe!"

My eyes snapped open, and a sharp breath caught in my throat as Liam's blood-curdling scream echoed in my ears.

Damn you, Rory. Just last night we'd been watching that old black-and-white vampire flick.

I lay in bed on my stomach, face pressed deep into the pillow.

I lay in bed, flat on my stomach, face buried in the

pillow.

"Phoebe!" someone shouted from inside my room. I bolted upright and turned to see Rory. "Were you in some kind of pie-eating contest in your sleep?"

"What?" I asked, squinting at him as he drew the curtains to let in bright sunlight.

"You were biting the hell out of your pillow and moaning," he added in disgust.

My cheeks burned with embarrassment as I lobbed a pillow his way. "What the hell are you doing here?"

"Waking you up for school. You're, like, fifteen minutes late. Plus, Mom's home—she's cooking breakfast."

I rolled my eyes; that meant family time was on the agenda. "I'll be down in a sec," I mumbled, sinking back into my pillow while replaying the dream before it turned bloody—the way Liam held me, moaning my name in a way that felt irresistibly sexy.

My chest fluttered, remembering the Looney Saloon was happening tonight.

I anxiously texted the girls about my ride with Liam knowing they would be all over that story.

Twenty minutes later, I plopped down at the kitchen

table. Mom stood at the stove, her back to us. Rory, already devouring pancakes, glanced up, and wiped syrup from his chin. Damn, he ate like a two-year-old.

"Who're you all dolled up for?" he sneered, puckering his lips to mimic my pink lip gloss. I snatched his orange juice and finished it. "Hey, I *wanted* that."

Mom turned at the fuss. "You look bright and beautiful today," she said, eyeing my yellow sundress. "Are you going to the beach?"

"Yeah, let a shark take a bite outta you," Rory said, before shoveling another fork of pancakes into his mouth.

"No. Just to school, and then to Laura's tonight."

Mom's eyebrow went up at that. "Oh yeah? Like a sleepover?"

I sighed. "I'll be back before curfew, so don't start lecturing me. I have to meet up with them, you know—now that I'm a member of their club. My God," I uttered under my breath. I *never* could hold a decent conversation with her without getting riled up. Dad and I got along so well. Mom constantly butted heads with me.

She set a plate of pancakes in front of me. "They're probably cold," she whispered.

I brushed the plate aside. "I'm not hungry, anyway.

Where's Rich?"

"He already left for work," Mom answered, a grin crossing her face. "I thought we could have a little bonding time without him."

Then why did we move in with him? I wanted to ask, but I swallowed my words. I couldn't wait to get away from that house. It was like the walls were closing in, trying to suck every breath of life out of me. Instead of walls, I should say Mom. I glared at her as she headed for the sink. If not for her short haircut, we'd be bookends with the same dirty blond-colored hair and olive eyes. Lately, she just seemed so worn out.

I drew my chair back and got to my feet, totally forgetting I was walking to school. I had to get a move on. Rory stared at me wide-eyed as he chewed slowly.

"You're leaving?" Mom cried.

"Yes. I'm already late," I muttered, stalking toward the hall.

"Okay, have a good day, Phoebe," Mom called, but I pretended not to hear her and slipped out the door.

"Let's see yours, Phoebe," Liam called later in class, as we had just thirty minutes to create a painting that told a story.

I eased to the front of the room, clutching my painting as if it were my lifeline.

"Go, Phoebe," Laura half-whispered from the front row. Her quiet encouragement, along with the smirks and giggles from the other girls—as they still buzzed about my joy ride with Liam—made it clear they couldn't believe my luck.

Standing before Liam's desk, he leaned casually against it beside me. One whiff of his cologne, and my knees buckled.

"Let's see it," he urged softly.

I shakily held it out to everyone. The entire sheet was taken up by a giant eyeball, complete with long lashes and a bold brow; its pupil swirled with a mix of colors, reminiscent of a rainbow.

"Beautiful, Phoebe. What does it mean?" Liam asked.

"She's gay?" someone from the back quipped, drawing chuckles from several students.

"Don't be insensitive," Liam snapped. "Go on, Phoebe."

I licked my lips. "People see only in shades of gray. This painting reflects my perspective of the world."

For a moment, Liam was speechless, his mouth agape. "That's very creative, Phoebe. Amazing." He applauded just as the bell rang, sending students leaping to their feet.

Liam approached me, leaning into my ear. "Would it be alright if I kept that?"

My heart skipped a beat. "S-sure," I managed to squeak out.

"I'd like to hang it here as a reminder for students to live as colorfully and freely as life itself. Please, sign and date it," he said, producing a pen for me. My fingers trembled as they added my initials—and in that moment, it became the *best* day of my life.

Our hands brushed as he accepted the painting. I longed for his eye contact, but he was too enamored with the artwork to look up. He carefully placed it on his desk before turning his attention elsewhere.

"Do you care to tell me what happened yesterday?" Miss G asked during our daily session in her office.

I sighed and shrugged. "It was just a misunderstanding. Thinking back on it, I overreacted." After all, Laura was the boss. I probably *shouldn't* have stepped on her toes like that. I appeared as a show-off to the rest of the cheerleaders—and that was not cool. Luckily, though, no one dwelled on it anymore. Laura and the others were way too excited about my Liam adventure. After visual arts, they lingered, waiting for me to break into that silly kid song, *Sitting in a Tree K-I-S-S-I-N-G*, their cheers and hoots so loud I was sure Liam could hear.

Miss G nodded, sympathetically. "You're entitled to a bad day. Just remember, when you do, take three deep breaths—the negativity will simply float away." She fluttered her fingers and then gestured to my dress. "By the way, you look *gorgeous* today. Is that to catch the eye of someone special?"

I blushed. "Not really. It's sorta stupid."

Miss G reached eagerly across the table. "You *have* to tell me who."

"It's just a crush, that's all—nothing serious."

She looked thoughtful for a moment, then said, "Oh, it's that new guy, Mr. Little?" scrunching her nose. "He's every girl's eye candy lately—I just don't get it."

"How can you *not*?"

"He's just too macho—and those tattoos..." she shuddered, then added, "though his nephew is absolutely adorable." She raised her eyebrows playfully.

I forced a smile. Ethan finally agreed to have a study date on Sunday. I still believe he sent me that *roses are red* text. I mean, his behavior was too suspicious. He kept our chat brief and avoided eye contact, as if burdened by guilt, perhaps over that threatening message.

Suddenly, someone burst into the office, causing me to jump in my seat in shock—Miss G did the same. It turned out to be Mr. Diggs. "Oh, I'm sorry, ma'am," he apologized, "I thought you'd already gone to lunch."

Miss G held a hand to her chest, chuckling. "Diggs, you scared me half to death!" She ducked under the table to grab her small waste basket.

Mr. Diggs trudged over with his head down to fetch it, barely acknowledging my presence in the room. No way he was responsible for the texts.

By eight that night, I stood before my mirror admiring my outfit—a black tube top, and denim short shorts. I had curled my normally straight hair and applied heavy eye makeup. With hoop earrings in place, I could easily pass for twenty-one. I tiptoed past Mom's room in my stiletto heels. This look hardly screamed *book club*.

As I inched down the hall, Taffy trotted over, barking excitedly. Dammit! I knew I'd been caught. Veering for the staircase, I took the stairs two at a time. The front door lay just within reach, so I closed my eyes and gripped the doorknob tightly. The coast was clear. Silently, I shut the door behind me and dashed across the driveway.

The Loony Saloon was a hole-in-the-wall shack downtown, its small parking lot crammed with trucks and motorcycles. I hadn't meant to park there; my plan was to linger near the back door, ready to slip inside whenever someone stepped out for a smoke. It sounded brilliant at first, but as I eased my car into the alley, reality hit—what were the odds anyone would actually *use* the back door?

Temptation to turn back and go home tugged at me, but then I spotted the blue truck. *Liam's truck*. Maybe if he noticed me, he'd let me in.

I pulled over near the dumpsters and turned off the engine. Muffled music thumped as I sat there, anxiously gripping the steering wheel. Minutes passed until I was about to give up when the back door opened and Liam stepped out. I hurriedly climbed from my car, my mind jumbling with potential words—I felt like a starstruck groupie at a concert, though Liam was just my teacher.

Liam soon tugged a blond out the door—an attractive figure in a short, tight-fitting black dress.

I lingered in the shadows near the stinky dumpster reeking of rotten food—it was disgusting as hell, yet I couldn't peel my eyes away from them.

They bumped against each other, giggling uncontrollably as her heels clicked on the pavement. Liam slid his hand onto her lower back, a gesture that echoed my vampire fantasy where he had touched me similarly.

Liam pressed her against the side of the building and hungrily kissed her. Her arms went up to his shoulders as she kissed him back. After a few seconds, they broke away to catch their breath, and as Liam stepped aside, the blonde's face came into view under a lamppost—I squinted to be sure.

Oh. My. God. *Miss G?*

7

pHoeBe

 as I was about to shut the door, Rich leaned out inquisitively.

"Back so soon?"

Keeping myself hidden behind the door, I replied, "Yep, I wanted to get a head start on my homework."

"K. Goodnight, Phoebe."

"Mm-hmm. See ya." I quickly shut the door and leaned against it. So much was going through my mind I didn't know where to begin. I'd never get to sleep, that's for sure.

Laura's accusations about Miss G now made perfect sense. What about Miss G's fiancé? She pretended Liam wasn't her type. How fake.

I stalked to the center of the room, kicking my shoes off along the way. How could I trust another word from Miss G after everything?

I knew the girls would never believe the story, but they'd sure as hell witness it—I'd recorded the teachers' entire quickie on my phone.

After tossing and turning, images of Liam and Miss G haunting my dreams, I finally rolled over, grabbed my phone, and sent the video to my group chat with Laura, Mimi, and Cassie. It was three in the morning, but who cared? I had to tell someone. The moment I hit SEND, the burning fire inside me simmered. I collapsed on my pillow and drifted back to sleep.

I awoke a little later, feeling as if the night—sneaking to the Loony Saloon, hiding by dumpsters, recording the video, and sharing it—had been one twisted dream. But when I checked my phone and was hit with a barrage of texts from the girls, I knew just how real it had been.

holy shit!

what a slut

I knew it

you actually witnessed that?

that cheating bitch

I dismissed the notifications, deciding to discuss it with the girls later, then leaned back against my pillow as my phone buzzed once more. It was that unknown number.

Daises are white, roses are red

Like your cut up torso when I kill you dead

I read it over and over. What the hell? Were they threatening to kill me?

Who the hell is this?

After a beat, they replied.

Your secret admirer

Yeah, right. I rolled my eyes. I wasn't about to waste another second on that idiot. I blocked the number immediately.

I talked to the girls that morning on a three-way call. Laura and Mimi were together, of course, while Cassie joined on the second line. After hours of gossiping about Liam and Miss G, I mentioned the creepy text. Cassie took my side—we didn't believe it was Diggs. Laura and Mimi weren't convinced. In the end, we all chalked it up to a lonely asshole who got off on prank-calling people. It didn't matter anymore since I'd blocked their number.

That afternoon, while picking up some supplies at the art store, I bumped into Zander in the parking lot.

"What are *you* doing here?" we both blurted out in unison.

I laughed and raised my bag. "Just grabbing some art supplies," I said, even though it was really just an excuse for adult coloring books I wasn't about to admit.

"Oh, okay, I just came from the gym," he said. He sported a red muscle tank and grey sweatpants, his blond hair pulled back into a neat ponytail.

I patted his defined bicep. "Nice seeing you," I said as I turned to leave, but he stopped me. I closed my eyes, already anticipating what he wanted next.

"Have you had lunch yet? There's a cozy diner just

nearby."

"Zander—" I started to decline his offer—but damn, I *was* hungry. I'd even skipped breakfast that morning. Seeing his expectant look, I shrugged. "Sure."

Nearly five minutes later, I followed Zander's Audi to a small diner called Ma's Table, famous for its chili, according to him.

After scanning the menu twice, that was my choice—their chili. "The chili and a Coke, please," I said to the server.

Zander glanced up from his menu. "Don't you mean diet Coke?"

I glared at him in disbelief. "Excuse me?"

He forced a laugh before turning back to the server. "I'll have a Caesar salad—no croutons, no dressing—a club chicken sandwich without mayo or bacon, and a bottled water." After she jotted down our order and hurried off, Zander looked at me and explained, "I just thought you'd want to monitor your calorie intake. Coach has the basketball team on a strict diet."

I nodded. Well, that made sense.

"I don't mind the discipline though," he continued, flexing his arms. "These guns are looking better than ever." I remained unimpressed as I glanced out the window.

The server returned with our drinks. "I'll be back shortly with your order."

I took a small sip of soda, and I swear I caught Zander wince.

"So, you're really into art?" he asked.

"*Yes*. I love oil paintings—especially masterpieces like the *Mona Lisa* and Van Gogh's *Starry Night*. That's real talent…" My voice fell flat. I could tell I lost him at oil painting.

"Is that what you want to do? Like after high school and stuff? I'm going to be a police officer. My sister's a cop, and she's filled me in on enough shit that I will ace the exam like that," he declared, snapping his fingers.

"Nice."

As we ate, our conversation shifted to the upcoming game. He told me about his pre-game ritual of petting his Newfoundland dog for good luck—a ritual he claimed had kept him undefeated.

"You're kidding. What's his name?"

"Lucky." We both laughed, and he reached across the table, taking my hand. "I'm really glad we got to hang out today."

I pictured Laura and slowly let go of his grip. "So, what happened between you and Laura?"

"Laura?" He repeated her name as if he'd never heard of her.

"Yes, your ex-girlfriend."

"I know. I just don't see why you're interested."

"Laura's my friend, Zander. You're her ex. See where I'm going?"

"Okay, but Laura doesn't rule my life. I can date whoever I please."

I chuckled. "Easy now—this is just *lunch*. Not a date."

"Fair point. Though dinner might count…?" He grinned, letting the possibility linger.

"We'll see."

He sank back into his seat with a smug smile just as a ruckus at the front of the diner grabbed our attention. A woman burst in, balancing a screaming kid on her hip. She was arguing with a server—a short blonde whose face I recognized. I leaned forward.

"Hey, that's Cassie," I cried, a bit too loudly. At the sound of her name, Cassie glanced up, her face flushed with embarrassment. In a flurry, she spun back to the woman and hurried her toward the door—I even thought I heard her call out, "Mom!" The woman, a brunette in tight jeans and a low-cut blouse spilling her cleavage, was now furiously pointing and yelling at Cassie. Eventually, Cassie managed to send her off.

"What the hell was that about?" Zander muttered as Cassie slowly made her way over.

"Hey!" I sprang to my feet and wrapped her in a hug.

"I didn't know you worked here," Zander said, a trace of disgust tinting his voice. I shot him a puzzled look— what difference did it make?

Cassie's cheeks went red. "Yeah. Just something to do." She nervously ran a hand through her hair. "My mom is driving me crazy, so I need to get out sometimes. It's only part-time."

"You mean that crazy woman a moment ago?" Zander butted in.

Cassie lowered her eyes. "That was her and my little brother. She expected me to babysit him during my shift. Can you believe it? Don't get me wrong. I love my baby brother very much—it's just that…"

I let my hand glide along her arm. "I'm sorry. Moms can be…"

"Yeah," she agreed before I could finish. Then she asked, "Hey, can I ask you something?" and motioned for me to step away from the table. Zander busied himself with his phone.

"Can you not tell the others about this?" she whispered once we were out of his earshot. Her blue eyes shimmered with anxiety. "I just don't want anyone to know I'm a server. You know how Laura and Mimi are—super rich and all."

"Of course, I won't say a word," I promised, trying to sound sincere even though Cassie blinked uneasily. "Don't worry about it, Cass. And if you ever need to talk, I'm here."

She brightened immediately. "I really appreciate that, Phoebe. Guess I'll get back to it now." She hurried away just as the manager stepped out and called her.

MIMI

"Oooh, I'm telling Papa!" My eleven-year-old sister, Bianca the Brat, stood in my doorway. Glancing over my shoulder, I quickly closed my laptop and chased after her. I caught her by the hair at the hall's end, and we tumbled to the floor, wrestling.

"You're not telling a soul," I warned, winding her long, dark strands around my hand.

She grinned devilishly. "Sure, I will." I tugged hard enough to snap her head back. "Ow!" she shrieked, eyes squinting in pain.

"*What* did I say?" I demanded through clenched teeth.

"Alright, I won't tell," she sobbed as I pulled her head again. "*Ow.* I *promise*, Mimi."

"Good." I let her go and scrambled to my feet. "If I ever catch you in my room again, I'm gonna cut out your tongue, you little bitch." I stormed back to my room, leaving her sobbing on the floor.

My cellphone buzzed on the pillow. Laura's sexy grin filled the screen, and *I* smiled, momentarily forgetting Bianca. "What's up?" I answered, dropping onto my bed in a dreamy haze.

"You won't *believe* this," Laura shrieked on the other end, her voice raw with emotion. Was she crying?

"What's wrong, L?" I asked, alarmed.

"Cassie just called me. She said Zander and Phoebe were on a *date* this afternoon."

I rolled my eyes. Of course, it's about Zander.

"That can't be happening. How dare Zander drop *me* for *her*? Like, what a downgrade. Do you know how many people will laugh at me once word spreads? Mimi, we *have* to do something!"

My heart ached at her distress. I sat up slowly, my mind scrambling for a way to calm her down.

"We'll figure something out, Laura. Just relax."

"Don't *tell me* to relax. I want that slut's *head* on a platter." I yanked the phone away from my ear, as she screamed like a maniac. When I returned it, she was saying something about picking up Phoebe tomorrow.

I listened, nodding silently as she detailed her scheme. By the time we hung up, she'd returned to her perky self. I shuffled over to my desk, sat in front of my laptop, and stared at my favorite picture of Laura. My bottom lip trembled.

It was tearing me apart that she couldn't move on from Zander. He could never love her the way I did.

8

pHoeBe

"CAN I GET YOU ANYTHING? SNACKS? SOMETHING to drink?" I offered Ethan on Sunday.

He shrugged. "Sure. Thanks." He sat on the sofa while I headed into the kitchen for refreshments. We had the house to ourselves—Mom and Rich were at a church meeting, and Rory was off doing whatever the hell Rory does.

I poured an entire bag of pretzels into a large bowl and grabbed two Cokes while replaying in my head how to bring up the texts with him. Part of me wanted to just let it go—I had already blocked the perpetrator—but I also needed to know if my hunch was right and, if so, why?

What had I done to deserve threats?

I returned to the den where Ethan was admiring photos on the mantel. He wore neon green cargo shorts and a black t-shirt.

"You look like your mom," he said, his back to me. I placed the snacks on the table with a frown. "It's not an insult," Ethan added, catching my sour face. "Your parents seem really nice."

"Yeah, well…" I plopped on the couch, taking a handful of pretzels with me. "That's not my father." He glanced up, surprised, his mouth forming a wide o. "Rich is my mom's boyfriend. My dad died last year." I exhaled deeply. It'd been a long time since I said those words out loud. Every time I did, it still hit me like I was hearing the bad news for the first time.

Ethan lowered himself beside me.

I slowly chewed a pretzel. "I was at school when I got the news. Mom didn't even wait for me to come home. They called me to the principal's office, where Mom explained Dad died in some sort of stick-up." I closed my eyes, picturing the faces surrounding me when I came to: Mom, the principal, the nurse, the secretary, and nearly the entire school peeking in from the hallway. I was the basket case—the girl everyone either pitied or mocked.

I leaned forward, resting my forearms on my knees, and laughed bitterly. "You wanna know the worst part? I started hallucinating about my dad. I couldn't—*wouldn't* accept he was gone. I had some sort of psychotic break, and then the hallucinations began. I saw my dad everywhere, alive and well." Immediately, I wished I could suck those words back into my mouth. I barely knew Ethan—hell, he was the top name on my suspect list for being a creep—but I spilled my life story to him.

Nice. Phoebe.

"But you got through all of that somehow," Ethan said.

"What makes you say that?"

He reached over and turned my hands so my palms were facing upward—revealing the scars. No one had ever done that before. I jerked my hands away and folded my arms tight against my middle.

"I don't mean to pry. It's just… well… I can relate." I slowly peeked at him. He tugged at his collar, exposing his left shoulder and an upper arm crisscrossed with white slashes—healed cut wounds. "I don't do that anymore. I mean, it was stupid in the first place, but I was everyone else's punching bag already, so I thought, why not?"

I didn't know what to say. Apologizing would've sounded lame. "Wait, does Liam… *hit* you?"

"Nah. Liam's been doing the best he can, I guess. He's not exactly guardian material, if you know what I mean."

I shifted uncomfortably, images of the Loony Saloon's alley flashing in my mind. *Oh, I know* exactly *what you mean,* I wanted to say, but instead I just nodded sympathetically.

"He's my mom's younger brother. She's… in prison."

I gasped. "Oh. Why? If you don't mind my asking."

"It's alright." He picked up a pretzel but didn't eat it—instead, he twirled it between his fingers. "My dad was an abusive asshole and one day… my mom killed him."

Wow. I was so not expecting *that.* I couldn't even begin to imagine it. My parents rarely argued, let alone fought.

Ethan gave me a sideways glance, pushing his glasses off his nose. "Hey, are we studying or in therapy?" he joked, his mouth curving into a crooked smile, though the emptiness in his eyes betrayed how he truly felt.

"Well, for what it's worth, you're the only person I've confided in about my past," I said. "Aside from my doc and counselor."

"Same here," he replied.

"So, if we ever need to talk about things, we can." I placed my hand on top of his, but he jerked it away scooted farther down the couch.

"I'm sure your *boyfriend* wouldn't be happy about that."

"Boyfriend? What boyfriend?"

"The blond with the perfect teeth."

"You mean, *Zander*? He's not my boyfriend." I burst into laughter. "Is *that* why you texted me those creepy Valentine poems?"

"What about a Valentine's poem?" He blinked, confusion written all over his face.

I playfully shoved him. "You can tell me."

He straightened his glasses again, looking me square in the eye. "I didn't text you anything, Phoebe." He was so sincere that I broke his gaze, feeling like an idiot. But then, if Ethan wasn't responsible, who was?

"I kept my distance from you because I didn't want you to make Zander jealous, catering to me and all." He stuck out his chin.

I smiled. "Okay—therapy's over. Let's study."

It was a little after five when Ethan left. I was about to make something for dinner when the doorbell rang.

"Hey, hey!" Mimi squealed.

"Mimi?" I sputtered, glancing past her to Laura in her Porsche, waving.

"Come on. Let's go shopping," Mimi said, excitedly tugging me out the door.

"Hey, camera girl," Laura said, glancing at me through the rearview mirror. I slid into the backseat with an eye roll, not wanting to *think* about Liam and Miss G. Laura giggled. "I'm so glad you confirmed what I knew all along. Miss G is not only a whore, but a two-timer. Like, what about her fiancé?"

Mimi clicked her seatbelt. "That poor bastard will never know. Miss G's gonna get away with it."

"Karma's a bitch and so is Miss G," Laura said. "She'll surely get what she deserves."

"Who cares?" I asked. "Where are *we* going? I'm starving."

"OMG," Mimi cried, whipping around in her seat. "We're going to Nichole's, the best jewelry store in Richmond."

"*Jewelry?*" I echoed.

"You have to see that place," Laura said. "It's unreal."

And Laura was not kidding. We got to Nichole's a

short while later. I had never seen so many diamonds in one place. I never cared about diamonds or fancy jewelry, though. Diamonds were Mom's thing. The most expensive piece I owned was a pair of gold post-earrings Dad got me on my thirteenth birthday. They were simple—like specks of gold in my lobes—and made me feel like a princess whenever I wore them.

"Here, check this out." Laura approached with a diamond-clustered choker. A bulbous ruby hung in the center. She held it against my neck. "My queen." Then she bowed.

Giggling, I did my best British accent. "Why, thank you, Lady Laura." We lingered at the necklace counter a while, trying on different pieces—a set of BFF necklaces caught our eye, though the price was outrageously high.

I shook my head. "Honestly, this stuff is way too expensive for me."

Laura peered at me through the mirror, a sly grin appearing on her face. "So take it," she whispered.

A small laugh escaped me. "What?"

Leaning in close, her voice low yet forceful, she said, "It's initiation week. You didn't think you'd get into the PLC that easily, did you?"

My heart slinked into my stomach. Was she *serious*?

Her brow arched challengingly, nodding for me to go on. "Let's go, Mimi."

I blinked at Mimi to say something, laugh, or even call Laura out—but Mimi simply followed Laura to the exit, her ponytail swishing behind her.

What the *hell*? I stood there dumbfounded, chewing on my lip. My eyes searched the ceiling for security cameras while my fingers toyed with the necklaces. There weren't any cameras—not that I could see. After a beat, I headed for the door without a necklace. Just as I reached the exit, though, I grabbed a pair of sunglasses off the display rack, and shoved the door open. A beefy hand clutched my shoulder, followed by a throat clearing. I glanced at the thick brown fingers, then up at the security guard's face. Where the hell had *he* come from?

"You need to come with me," he said, guiding me back inside.

My brain jumbled for an excuse. "I can explain—I swear—" was all I managed as he caught me red-handed. The security guard quietly led me to a small back room outfitted with TV screens showing every angle of the tiny store. *Shit*. "I'm so sorry. I was only going to—"

"The manager wants a word with you," the security guard said. Suddenly, as if emerging from the shadows, the manager appeared, arms folded across his chest. I peered at his face, and my knees buckled.

"*Dad?*"

9

pHoeBe

MOM SAT ACROSS FROM ME IN THE DEN AS RICH paced behind her seat later that night. After seeing Dad—or at least, *thinking* I saw him—I fainted. When I came to, Mom and Rich were there, along with security and a manager who looked nothing like Dad.

The manager took pity on me when I blacked out and decided not to press charges, but they banned me from the store. Not that I ever planned to go back anyway.

Mom folded her arms across her as she glared at me, tight-lipped. "What were you *thinking*, Phoebe?"

I didn't reply. What *could* I say? I knew right from wrong. Laura didn't hold a gun to my head and force me to steal—so why did I do it? Was I trying to prove myself?

Rory sat on the couch beside me, nervously chewing on his nail.

"You've never done something like that before. Why now? Did somebody put you up to it? Like some sort of initiation?"

"No," I muttered. Yes—but I couldn't admit that otherwise, she'd take it to Principal McGee. I'd get kicked out of the PLC. Hell, the PLC might even get into trouble or, worse, get disbanded. No way was *I* gonna be responsible for that. I straightened up and stared Mom in her flushed face. "I was gonna pay for the sunglasses. I just had to grab my wallet."

"That's bullshit, and you know it, Phoebe," Rich exploded, making Rory shift in his seat. "Do you have any idea how embarrassing it was when the officers—my fellow officers—called and said my girlfriend's daughter got caught stealing?"

My face twisted in disgust. "I don't care that you're embarrassed. You don't have to be here."

Rory snickered.

"Watch it," Mom ordered. "And that isn't the point either, Rich. The fact is, you stole, Phoebe." She sighed. "Rich and I have talked it over, and we want you to get a job."

"What?"

Mom nodded. "Yes. Maybe all these luxuries are making you too comfortable. We don't want you to—"

"Wait, are you trying to say I'm *spoiled*? I don't give a shit about Rich's money."

"Then you shouldn't mind earning your own," Rich spat at me.

Mom raised her hands. "Let's not forget what this is all about. You committed a crime, Phoebe. You're lucky they didn't charge you."

"Yeah, thanks to me," Rich said.

That was the last straw. I spun toward him. "Why are we having this discussion with you, Rich? Can't I talk to Mom privately? My business doesn't concern you."

Rich's eyes bulged. "Doesn't concern me? I kept you from being arrested. Do you have any idea how colleges would've reacted to *that* on an application?"

"Why do you care? You're not my fucking father."

"And just what do you think your father would say?"

I jumped to my feet. "Don't you dare. You have no right to speak about Dad when you're with his wife." I shot Mom a dagger look.

"Dad died believing you were his best friend—you committed the ultimate betrayal. You'll never be the man my father was. Not even close."

"Stop this—*right* now," Mom commanded, glaring at us both.

"No, Diane. It's time she knows."

"Rich!" Mom stood up.

Rich stalked around to me. Mom tried to block his path, but he eased her aside. "The ultimate betrayal, you say. You have no idea what that means. Nor do you know the man your father was."

"He was a whole lot better than you, Rich," I said, wrapping my arms in front of me, glaring at him coldly.

Rich leaned inches from my face. "David was a corrupt cop, Phoebe. He stole money, sold drugs. He was under investigation and was about to go to jail. That's why he *killed himself.*"

His words punched me in the gut. "*What?*" I staggered backward, completely winded.

"Rich, you bastard," Mom hissed. Rich's shoulders heaved as he, too, rasped for breath. "*Go.*" Mom ordered him. Rich moved away from us, but he didn't leave the room. "Phoebe—" Mom reached for me, but I swatted her hands away.

"Dad committed suicide? Why did you lie to me?"

Mom covered her face with her hands for a beat before facing me. "I'm so sorry, honey. I was going to tell you but after you…" She shook her head, unable to finish. "I thought I'd lost you, too. I didn't know how to tell you afterward. I'm so sorry." She wrapped her arms around me, forcing me into a tight embrace.

"No. *No*. Dad would never leave me like that. He could never leave us!"

"I knew you wouldn't understand it then, Phoebe," Mom said, gripping me tighter.

"Stay away from me. I hate you. I hate you both!" I broke free from her hold.

She reached for me again. "Phoebe, *please*."

Sobs ripped from Rory as he bolted from the room. I hurried after him, catching him on the landing.

"It isn't fair!" he cried into my shoulder between muffled sobs. "How could Dad do that to us?"

My swollen throat refused to form any words.

After sitting with Rory until he fell asleep, I slipped inside my room and shut the door. It was five minutes until midnight. Mom and Rich had been arguing for the past hour. When things finally quieted, I crept over to my bed and turned out the lights just as one of them rapped at my door.

"Phoebe?" It was Mom. "Are you awake?" She knocked once more. After several seconds, I heard her walk away, and then the door closed to their bedroom.

Rich must have been sleeping on the couch. I rolled my puffy eyes and swiped at my burning nose. The truth they'd revealed gave me a splitting headache. I sat on the edge of my bed, the moonlight playing peek-a-boo through my curtain, as I grasped memories. It made sense though—why Dad hugged me so tightly the last time I saw him, and how he promised everything would be okay. He knew he was leaving me.

My lip quivered, and I broke into a quiet cry. After a beat, my cell buzzed, interrupting the silence. I fumbled around in the dark for it and discovered dozens of texts from Laura, Mimi, Zander, and Ethan.

Ethan's was from just a minute ago.

Today's session was awesome.

Sniffing, I thumbed—

Can you come over?

You gotta sneak up to my window

The last one in back

Ethan replied—

Be there in a sec

Sighing, I switched on the flashlight feature on my phone, sat it face-down on the bed, and waited patiently for Ethan. I collapsed onto my pillow, exhausted, after twenty minutes had passed, when a tap at the window alerted me. It was Ethan. I hurriedly raised the window to let him in.

"Sorry, I took so long. I rode my bike," Ethan whispered as he carefully lowered one leg inside, then the other. His feet landed softly on the carpet. I shuffled zombified steps to my bed and plopped down. Ethan hovered near the window, nervously fidgeting with his fingers. "Are you okay?" he asked in a low voice. Shoulders sagging, I shook my head. Ethan carefully approached. "I'm gonna sit down if that's alright," he said, settling beside me. He carried the scent of a rainforest—fresh linen mingled with the outdoors. We sat there in silence for a moment, the flashlight beam dancing on the ceiling.

"All that time I believed my dad died honorably, only to find out he killed himself." My voice shook, and my whole body trembled with sadness, anger—rage. "He committed suicide, and everyone *lied* to me about it." I turned and buried my face in his shoulder, tears pouring from me like a broken faucet. "My dad was a crook," I hiccupped.

My chest felt like it was splitting wide open. "Everything hurts... *so* bad," I whispered, my shoulders trembling with each sob.

Ethan gently wrapped an arm around me. "Your dad made his choice. Maybe taking his own life was his way of righting his wrongs. Or perhaps he cared about his family too much to drag you all into his mess.

"You can't hurt yourself over what happened or how it happened. In the end, it won't change a thing or bring your father back."

"I know," I wailed. I pressed against Ethan's arm, his shirt sleeve now soaked with my tears. He continued to stroke my hair gently, the gesture calming me until my eyes grew drowsy. I can't say how long we sat like that, but as my body relaxed against him, I eventually fell into a deep sleep.

I awoke hours later, alert, reminded that Ethan was still there. Groggily, I sat up—my head pounding and my entire body sore. I was under the covers, still in my jeans and T-shirt. Even the bright sunlight streaming in stung my eyes. I squinted through the light for Ethan, but he wasn't there. The window was open, with the curtain flapping in the breeze.

Memories of yesterday replayed in my mind. The jewelry store. Hallucinating about Dad. Mom and Rich. The *truth* about Dad. Ethan's comforting words. I hated myself for calling him over, only to fall asleep. I longed to crawl back under the covers and never emerge, but I couldn't bear another minute with Mom and Rich.

Swinging my feet to the floor, I edged to the side of the bed—and that's when I saw it. My usually blank canvas had been transformed: a beautiful rose painted on it, with fat blue water droplets glistening on its red petals. In elegant black handwriting, it read:

There may be showers in the forecast today, but the sun

always returns, shining brighter and ready to dry away your tears

I felt like melting. Ethan's words offered a glimmer of calm, as if everything would eventually be okay—even though deep down, I knew that wasn't the case.

The rest of my classes passed in a blur, like one of those *Twilight Zone* episodes where everything zips by at super speed. I wasn't even sure if Rory had made it to school; when I left, he'd still been in bed. Rich sat on the couch in the den, and Mom only made herself a cup of coffee, no pancakes. Neither of us spoke a word. What could anyone say? They'd lied to me enough already.

"Phoebe, I hope you heard what I said," Mrs. Peters called out as the bell rang, startling me.

I blinked at her in confusion. Mrs. Peters was the trig teacher. "Uh, sure," I muttered, gathering my books and standing up. She watched me cautiously as I headed for the door.

"Phoebe, girl! What happened?" Laura asked, catching up with me in the hall. Her dark curls were neatly pulled into a bun. "Were you arrested?"

Cassie approached and gasped. "Arrested for what?"

"We went to Nichole's," Mimi said.

"Without me?" Cassie pouted.

"Shut *up*, Cass," Laura snapped, nudging her aside. "Phoebe has to tell us what happened."

But my mind couldn't recall anything beyond the bombshell Rich had dropped: *Dad killed himself*. He'd once promised me everything would be alright, and then he ended his life. How *could* he?

"Hello?" Mimi teased, pretending to knock on my forehead. I had to shut my eyes to keep my tears away.

"Oh, honey, I'm sorry," Laura said, enveloping me in a hug. "I didn't mean to get you into trouble. I didn't think you'd actually *steal* the necklaces."

I sniffled, pulling myself together. "I didn't… get into trouble, I mean. My mom's boyfriend is a detective."

Laura's eyes flashed. "I didn't know that." She shot Mimi a glance before smiling. "Anyway—" She rummaged through her backpack and pulled out three tiny velvet boxes. "One for you," Laura said, handing a box to Mimi. "And one for you," she added, giving me a box.

"Aww, *L*," Mimi squealed, revealing one of the gold

BFF necklaces.

I opened my box and had FOREVER. "Wow. Thank you, Laura."

Laura beamed with pride. "I felt guilty about what happened and went back to buy them."

"They're really cute," Cassie remarked, peering over my shoulder at the necklaces.

"Hey, ladies," Miss G's voice called from behind.

My heart skipped a beat—I hadn't seen her since the Loony Saloon's alley incident.

"Hi, Miss G!" Laura and Mimi chorused, exchanging secretive glances. Cassie waved with a smug grin.

"Hey there, Phoebe," Miss G said, gently touching my shoulder as she came into view.

I shifted uncomfortably and forced a smile. "Hi," I croaked.

"See you at noon?" she asked, referring to our daily session.

"Oh, I have to skip today. I've got a makeup test in pre-calc due," I said, totally lying.

Miss G tried to hold my gaze, searching for any sign of truth, but I stared past her at the lockers. The bustling students. *Liam*. He was approaching, eyes fixed ahead.

"Hi, Mr. Little!" Laura called out, drawing attention.

Liam smiled and nodded at us, completely ignoring Miss G.

"Well, hopefully, we get together sometime today," Miss G said, patting me on the back before she and Liam went in opposite directions.

Mimi giggled as she watched Miss G leave. "They're totally crushing on each other."

"Uh-uh," Laura replied, shaking her head. "I think that's long past."

I couldn't give two shits about them.

At lunch, I sat gloomily at the cheerleaders' table, scanning for Ethan but finding no sign of him—and he hadn't replied to any of my texts. Maybe he'd slept in after waiting up with me all night.

The girls' giggling pulled me back to focus on my plate of macaroni and cheese. Just as I took a bite, Zander slid into the seat beside me.

"You're a hard person to catch," he remarked, seating himself on the bench with a leg hanging casually over each side. His shiny silver cycling t-shirt accentuated his muscular, action-figure build.

Mimi cleared her throat. "Excuse you, but don't you have your own table—the one for morons?"

Zander flashed her a smile as he grabbed my hand underneath the table. I struggled to maintain my composure as I freed myself, catching a blank look from Laura as she forked through her food.

I blinked at Zander, at the way his silver top clashed with his blond hair. "What's up?"

"French," he answered simply. "For dinner. You can't be allergic to that." He tucked a strand of my hair back into place.

I really should've brushed my damn hair. "Um—I don't care for French cuisine," I said, stomach souring. Why mention that in front of Laura? I shot him a glare, hoping he would pick up on it.

"Japanese?"

"Can we talk about that later?" I whispered, struggling to keep down the bile rising in my throat. Between the loud chatter and Zander's demanding presence, my brain felt like it was *pulsing*.

When the last bell rang and school was finally out, I was desperate to get home and burrow back under the covers.

I collected my things from the locker, keeping my head down to avoid everyone, though everyone was too absorbed in their cell phones anyway. It was weird—like something from a horror movie, where everyone suddenly goes into a trance and freezes. They were huddled around their screens, whispering and giggling.

I slammed my locker shut, and Summer stepped out from behind it, her eyes narrowed in suspicion.

"You *lied* to me," she accused.

"Huh?"

"You said you weren't on social media."

"I'm not."

"Well, how did you post this?" Summer demanded, holding out her phone. I stared at the screen, at the footage of Miss G and Liam in the alley.

10

pHoeBe

I TREMBLED WITH RAGE. "THAT IS NOT MY account."

"But it says *Queen Bee Hall*, and it even has your photo on it. Look." Summer tried forcing her phone in my face, but I brushed it aside.

"I know what it says, but it isn't mine," I snapped. I spun around, panic rising as I realized everyone must have seen the video. Sweat beaded on my forehead. I broke away from Summer and pushed through the cluster of gossiping students. Reaching Laura at her locker, I slammed its door, barely missing her hands. "Laura, what the fuck?"

Her smile slowly faded as she met my intense stare. "Why are you so upset?"

"Upset?" My voice elevated an octave. "I'm *pissed*! How could you post that video—using that phony account in *my* name? What the *fuck*?" I slapped her locker door again.

"Take it easy, Phoebe," Mimi said, placing a hand on my shoulder. "It was just a joke."

"Well, I'm not laughing. Why would you post it in my name?"

Laura held up her hands defensively. "Duh, *you* recorded it—I couldn't steal your thunder, girl."

"I showed you guys that in confidence," I hissed, leaning in close to her.

"Phoebe, you need to relax," she replied.

"Delete it. *Right now*," I demanded.

With a sigh, Laura whipped out her phone, tapped the screen a few times, and turned it toward me. "There. Done. The video's gone, and the account is deleted. Now, can you chill the hell out?"

"No, I'm not going to let it slide." I jabbed a finger at her. "You threw me under the bus, and that's not cool at all."

Laura pressed her lips together and looked away sheepishly.

But Mimi glared at me. "If you didn't want anyone seeing the video, Phoebe, why did you record it?" she demanded, arms crossed.

"It was for us!" I spat. "*Our* secret. Now everyone…" Oh my God—*Ethan*. Did he see the video, too? Is that why he hasn't answered my texts? I spun around and bolted for the double doors, desperate to find him and explain.

"Phoebe, I'm sorry!" Laura called after me.

I raced out into the parking lot, scanning for Ethan. Maybe I'd drive around and search for him. My heart felt like a hand squeezed it as I surveyed the lot before heading to my car. But then, there Ethan was, unlocking his bike at the bike station.

"Ethan, wait!" I called, hurrying over. He was wearing his helmet but removed it when I approached. "I didn't know you were in school today—you didn't answer my texts. Are you okay?" My words tumbled out.

"I'm fine. How are you?" he replied, stepping closer while clutching his helmet. The lot grew busier and louder as students poured out.

Glancing behind me, I saw Mimi and Laura standing

together, watching us, with Zander nearby as well. "Can we go for a walk?" I asked.

"Sure." He hung his helmet on the bike's handlebars, slipped his hands into his jean pockets, and fell in step beside me. We walked across the street to a park bench that faced away from the school.

"I thought you were mad at me," I finally said.

"Mad at you for what?"

I looked at him, feeling partly relieved and mostly anxious—he hadn't heard about the video yet. I licked my dry lips, unsure where to begin. "Have you checked your phone lately?"

"Well, I left it at home. I didn't even have time to charge it after spending the night with you," he blurted, gasping. "I didn't mean…"

I smiled softly. "I loved your painting by the way. It warmed me inside and out." Ethan beamed with pride, though he said nothing. "But there's something I need to tell you," I continued, shamefully recounting the details about the video clip. His face remained blank. "What are you thinking, Ethan?"

He adjusted his glasses. "I'm not surprised—especially with Liam. He made his bed, so he's got to lie in it. Don't beat yourself up."

"I never wanted the video to get out. Laura—" I muttered, shaking my head.

"Yeah. She's some BFF," he remarked sarcastically, glancing at my necklace.

I rolled my eyes, fidgeting with the charm. I exhaled deeply, relieved to have told him the truth. "So, why didn't I see you in class?"

"Probably because you were too busy with your clique," he replied.

"My clique?"

"I saw you at lunch with *not-your-boyfriend*," he said, flashing air quotes.

I laughed. "You were there? Why didn't you come over? We could've—"

"Are you kidding me? Just go to the popular table and pull up a chair. It's that simple."

"Well, yeah. I would've introduced you to every—"

"I don't belong with them, Phoebe," he said firmly.

"You just don't know anyone yet," I insisted.

He raised his eyebrows and scoffed. "Oh, I know their type well. They're spoiled, conceited, and will burn anyone to get what they want. I dealt with types like that at my old school. They were the ones who…" He trailed off, his chest swelling with each breath.

I squeezed his shoulder gently. "Nobody's going to hurt you, Ethan. My friends aren't like those kids."

He stared off, keeping his eyes low. "I just hate them," he spat through clenched teeth. I wasn't sure if he meant my friends or the bullies from his old school, but something was clearly upsetting him. His grip on the bench tightened until his knuckles blanched. "I don't belong with them, and neither do you."

I frowned. "What's that supposed to mean?"

"It means that you're too kind for their clique," he replied. He shot me a sidelong glance. "I guess I don't know you that well, either," he admitted. "Maybe if we spent time together outside of our study sessions…" I grinned and playfully shoved him.

"Alright, well, the next time you call me over, can we at least use the front door? I swear, your bushes felt like a dozen thorns in my ass."

I laughed. "Deal." I extended my hand, and he took it, twisting it so that our fingers intertwined. It felt like electricity pulsing through my veins. I leaned back against his shoulder, and we sat in silence. It was the most peaceful and serene moment I'd experienced in ages. I longed to forget everything. The incident at Nichole's. The truth about Dad, the Liam and Miss G scandal. Yet, in the end, that was my reality.

———

Dr. Landry was an older man, his deep wrinkles reminding me of a Shar-Pei dog. He studied me intently, his gray eyes scanning every inch of me as if I were a lab rat under a microscope. It made me miss my sessions with Miss G.

I shifted, feeling my heart sink into my stomach. Four days had passed without a word from Miss G. Her family and friends had even turned to the media, pleading for any information about her whereabouts. How could someone simply vanish? The last anyone heard from Miss G was the day that video circulated—the video *I'd* recorded. The rumors were flying around school that Miss G was pregnant with Liam's baby.

Liam continued to show up at school daily, despite the gossip and snickers. Just that morning, he was locked in a heated conversation with Principal McGee. Laura joked that Principal McGee was upset about having competition, still convinced he was involved with Miss G, too.

I no longer cared about the details of Miss G's personal life. She had been the kindest, most loving person I'd met since coming to Richmond Heights, and I'd give anything to have her back—alive and well—for another heart-to-heart conversation.

After our explosive confrontation, Mom had scheduled an appointment with Dr. Landry, since it had been over a month since our last session. I figured I *needed* a follow-up visit—especially after I'd confused the jewelry store manager for Dad, though I hadn't mentioned that to Mom. Dr. Landry did his best to explain the incident.

"You're accustomed to calling your father during times of trouble," he said. "In that moment, overwhelmed with distress, you wanted him to come protect you. And you understand that it was all in your head, right?" He tapped his temple with a pen. I wasn't sure if he was asking or stating, so I simply nodded. I was just grateful he didn't treat my episode as a sign to guzzle pills again.

After shaking hands, I stood to leave.

"Phoebe?" he called.

"Yes?" I answered, a hint of impatience in my tone.

He pushed his glasses up his nose with his pinkie. "Call

me if you ever need anything—anything at all."

"Thank you, Dr. Landry. I'll keep that in mind." I forced a smile, though inside, I was desperate to leave. I maintained a steady stride out of his office, pausing only at the elevators to catch a deep, relieving breath. I always left his office feeling exposed—as if, no matter how hard I tried to conceal my emotions, he could always unearth them. After all, that *was* his job.

My phone pinged as the elevator opened.

What the *hell*? I glared at the text—from an unknown number:

> Roses are red, violets are blue

> I sharpened my knife just for you

That asshole was back. Annoyed, I shoved my phone into my pocket and hurried outside. It was a dreary day; there wasn't a sign of sun, only dark clouds threatening rain. As I spotted my car, a familiar voice called my name from across the street. I instantly recognized the blond hair—Zander.

I glanced back at the building I'd just left, searching desperately for another reason to have been there.

"Hey," Zander greeted as he hurried over, dressed in a navy-blue muscle shirt over khaki shorts.

"What's up, Zander?" I asked impatiently, fumbling in my purse for my car keys.

"Coming from the police station."

"Oh?" I raised a brow.

"My sister's at that precinct," he said, pointing across the street.

I hadn't even noticed a police station was nearby; its presence made my stomach churn. Memories of surprising Dad at his precinct as a child—bringing baked cookies, handmade cards, or drawings—flashed through my mind. His face always lit up as if he hadn't seen me in ages.

And he had been a corrupt cop. I turned away from the station bitterly.

As if sensing my inner turmoil, Zander arched an eyebrow. "You think you have what it takes to be an officer?"

I glanced back at my car, its bug eyes almost pleading for me to hop in and drive away. I so wanted to. I certainly wasn't in the mood for career advice.

"Anyway," he said before I could find my words,

"where are you headed?"

My fingertips brushed over the car keys. "Home," I answered woodenly. Before he could protest, I added, "I've got errands to run for my mom."

Hurt flashed across his face, but I didn't care. After the session with Dr. Landry and my worry over Miss G, all I craved was to lie down. I knew Mom would linger, eager to hear if I'd been prescribed anything, so I wanted nothing more than to avoid her brooding stare.

"Okay. Well, take care," Zander said, forcing a smile. He stepped back so I could pass. "See you at school."

I nodded and quickened my pace. The wind was chilly—the last thing I wanted was to get caught in the rain. As I neared my car, I sensed something was off. It was tilted at an odd angle. My stomach knotted as I circled around and stared in shock at the back tires: both had been slashed!

Who would do that? And who the hell had followed me to Dr. Landry's office?

Raindrops now splattered over my head and shoulders. With a shudder, I moved to the trunk to grab the spare Rich kept inside. I had learned to change a tire from Dad when I was fourteen—always his little helper, watching and learning. But I didn't know him at all, did I?

I popped the trunk open and was immediately hit by a foul, pungent odor. What the hell was that? Clenching my churning stomach, I lifted the lid—and screamed. A raccoon's lifeless, beady eyes stared up at me. Its fat, furry body had been slit open from neck to belly, its bloody insides spilling out into the trunk. I screamed again, staggering backward.

"Phoebe?" Zander called.

"Oh my God, Zander!" I spun around. He rushed back, and I fell into his embrace as tears mixed with the pounding rain.

"What's wrong?" he asked, holding me tightly.

"My *car*," I managed between trembling shakes of rage. "Somebody vandalized my car!"

Zander told me to wait while he went to investigate. I stood there in the pouring rain, my clothes clinging to my skin. I watched as he first examined the tires and then staggered in horror at the gruesome sight in my trunk. My hand clenched into a fist—who could be so callous as to hurt an innocent animal? I thought of Taffy—always chirpy and energetic, his tail wagging nonstop. Whoever did this was a monster.

Zander returned. "You should file a police report. Come on—my sister can help you."

About a half-hour later, with my hair damp and Zander's varsity jacket draped over my shoulders, I sat across from Officer Bridges. She was practically Zander's twin—same dreamy eyes, perfect tan, sparkling teeth—but her blond hair was cut in a dramatic style. She carefully took down my statement as I recounted every detail about my car. Another officer worked on disposing of the raccoon and doing whatever else cops do. Officer Bridges explained that without any concrete evidence, there wasn't much they could do, though they would tow the car to a garage for repairs. "Can I give you a ride home?" she offered.

"I can take her," Zander interjected.

Officer Bridge's eyes surveyed me. "Will that be okay with you?"

I didn't mind who drove as long as I got home. "Sure."

She smiled warmly. "I'm sorry about what happened. There are a lot of crazies out there today. Just remember to park near the cameras next time—at least we can review the footage to track down a suspect."

"Thanks a lot, Officer Bridges," I said, standing up and

shaking her hand.

She beamed. "It's a pleasure to meet Zander's new girlfriend under such unfortunate circumstances. I've heard so much about you."

New girlfriend? I shot a glance in Zander's direction. A stupid smile was frozen on his face. His sister said something about having me over for dinner to meet their parents when Zander cut in.

"Alright, Jenna, we've got to get going now," he said, squeezing my hand a bit too tightly as he tugged me toward the door. Outside, he let go and cleared his throat nervously. "So, uh, your place then?"

"Please?"

He led me to his royal blue Audi, and I slumped into the passenger seat, clutching his jacket around me.

"I can turn on the heat if you like," he offered.

"It's okay," I replied; in that moment, all I wanted was to figure out who my tormentor was. Text messages were one thing—but vandalizing my car, invading my personal space, was another.

I closed my eyes, sinking further into the warmth of his jacket. Whoever was behind this, I hoped they'd back off. Rich would have my *head* if he found out about the car.

"I'm sorry about what Jenna just said," Zander remarked. I straightened and looked at him; he kept his eyes on the road, one hand gripping the steering wheel tightly, the other tapping his knee nervously. "She just misunderstood, that's all," he added with a sidelong glance.

I shrugged it off. "Your sister is nice."

"Not as nice as me," he quipped with a wink.

Though I smiled, an uneasy feeling churned deep in my stomach as I rubbed my throbbing temples.

"Headache?" he asked.

"I can't make sense of this shit," I exclaimed. "Someone broke into my car, left a butchered animal, and slashed my tires. What are they trying to say?" I gasped. "Shit—the text." I recalled the message about a sharp knife. Slashed tires, a dismembered animal—did that mean I was next?

"Text?" Zander echoed. I shifted to him and spilled all the details. With every gruesome word, his face twisted into a frown. "Do you want to go back and report all that to my sister?"

I whipped out my phone. "I'm just gonna tell this

asshole to fuck off," I said as I scrolled to the unknown number and hit CALL. Forcing my trembling hand to steady, I held the phone to my ear as it began to ring. My heart knocked against my ribcage. Then, in the silence, I heard it—a low buzzing sound coming from somewhere inside the car. I blinked at Zander, still gripping the phone to my ear.

"Where's that sound coming from?"

"Huh? What sound?" he replied, clutching the steering wheel with both hands, tapping it nervously.

When no one answered, I hung up, and the buzzing ceased.

My veins went cold. I dialed the unknown number again, and the hum started again.

11

pHoeBe

I SLOWLY TURNED TO ZANDER. HE KEPT HIS EYES locked straight ahead, his body tense, sweat gleaming along the edge of his hairline.

"It's *you?*" I uttered in disgust.

He laughed nervously. "What's me? What are you talking about?"

"Answer the *phone*, Zander."

"What phone? *Hey!*" he cried, as I reached for his pockets. "Stop! What are you doing?" The car wove in and out of its lane. Grunting, I tried to slip my hand into his pockets, but he blocked me with a powerful forearm.

"Phoebe, *stop*." He swerved the car off the road, and

we came to a jolting halt near an open grassy field—in the middle of nowhere.

"What the hell is going on, Zander?" I demanded, my back pressed against the door.

"*Fine.*" He spun around, dug into his pocket, and produced a burner phone.

My jaw dropped. "Why would you *do* that? Text me those disgusting things?"

If his face could have reddened any further, it might have oozed blood. "I-I'm sorry. Believe me." He reached for me, but I moved away. The door handle dug into my skin, shooting a sharp pain up my back. His eyes dropped in shame. "You kept *blowing* me off, Phoebe. It pissed me off so much that I just wanted to get back at you. I swear that's it. I wasn't going to physically hurt you."

I swatted at him. "Are you fucking crazy?"

"I'm so sorry, Phoebe. I am. I wanted you to give me a chance…" His voice broke.

"I did! We had lunch. I was polite to you, Zander, and you terrorize me?" Gasping, my hand flew to my mouth. "That *poor* raccoon. You… you…" I couldn't gather my words as bile bubbled in the back of my throat.

"Now, wait a minute. That damn thing was already

dead when I found it. It was roadkill."

As if *that* justified his actions. "You're sick, Zander. Take me back to the police station. You need to tell them what you've done."

"Like hell, I will. Let's not blow this shit out of proportion. I admitted to you I did it. There's no reason to involve the cops. I didn't physically hurt you—I wouldn't." He reached to stroke my hair, but I slapped his hand away.

"Don't you ever touch me."

His eyes flared. "Why? Because you're fucking that weirdo Ethan?"

"*What*? That is *none* of your business."

As if he'd gotten his answer, he shook his head with a small laugh. "You goddamn slut," he spat, angrily swiping at my hair.

"What is wrong with you? You need to turn this car around and go back to the police station. Tell your sister the truth."

"I'm not telling anybody anything. And neither are you," he retorted, pointing at me.

"Why not?"

"Who will believe a word you say given your current

circumstances?"

I crossed my arms, my throat drying up. Did he know I was seeing a shrink? "What are you talking about, Zander?"

"You think I don't know what you've been up to? Stealing from Nichole's? Spying on your teachers? Wherever you go, the drama follows. Your credibility is falling apart if you try to pin shit on me. Everyone will think you're making it up for attention. For all anyone knows, you bought the burner phone and texted yourself," he said, reclining lazily in his seat with a satisfied smirk.

I stared back in utter disbelief, my arms dropping to my lap. "You've thought all of that through? There is no way you're getting away with this." I reached for the door handle but paused to face him. "Just so you know, it's impossible for a girl to take you seriously, Zander. You're arrogant, a control freak, and, above all, an asshole."

With an angry cry, he grabbed me by both sides of my face. "You bitch!" he screamed, pressing his palms into my jaw.

"Let go of me!"

"You're pathetic." His face screwed up in disgust, but

then he *kissed* me. His lips slammed against mine, his tongue forcing its way inside.

Panic surged through my chest. I couldn't breathe. My arms thrashed, clawing at the air. I grabbed his wrists, struggling to turn my face away, but his grip tightened—his nails digging into the flesh behind my ears. Tears blurred my vision as he kissed me hungrily, his teeth scraping against my bottom lip, and blood stung my tongue.

I clamped my hands around his wrists and drove my knee as high as I could into his stomach. He released my head and staggered backward. With a laugh, he reached for me again, but I slammed my foot into his chest. He crashed against his door hard, his head banging against the window.

"Ow!" he cried, gingerly touching his temple. My chest heaved as I struggled to calm down. My sore cheeks were wet with tears. He spun toward me, one eye half-closed. I screamed as he grabbed me, tearing at the varsity jacket.

"Give me back my jacket," he demanded, tugging as I tried to strip it off. "Get the fuck out of my car."

I fumbled for the door until it popped open and dropped into a puddle of mud. Zander reached to shut the door, and within seconds, the blue Audi sped away. I climbed to my feet, trembling, my lips sore and swollen. Clutching my purse tightly to my chest, I staggered along the road, sobbing like a baby.

MIMI

I sat on the edge of Laura's bed, painting my toenails as I watched her pace the plush carpet—a pace that raised the possibility of setting a fiery trail—while she ranted about Phoebe, of course.

She paused to glare at me. "Her mom's fucking a detective? How come I didn't know about that?"

"Don't look at me. I know no more about her than you do."

"Why is that? Why don't we know about her? Where did she come from? What are her secrets? Where, what, why?" She tilted her head back and screeched.

I laughed. Laura sounded like an evil villain from a Disney movie. "Maybe she's just untouchable. Perhaps you can't beat her, L," I said, carefully painting my baby toe.

"Did you see the way she came at me—about the

video?" Laura stopped in front of her mirror and, with a hoarse cry, punched it. The mirror cracked, but none of its pieces fell.

"Dammit, Laura." I jumped to my feet, hurrying to check how badly she'd hurt herself.

"Nobody talks to me like that!"

I sighed. "Everybody gets pissed off once in a while," I muttered under my breath as I examined her hand. Bits of shard pricked her flesh, so I reached for my manicure kit and tweezers.

"No—everyone has weaknesses, fears, flaws. She isn't perfect. She fucks up just like the rest of us. Posting that video proved it. Liam and Miss G both know that their favorite student can be a *bitch*."

"Mm-hmm," I muttered, going along while tending to her hand. As I plucked away at the mirror bits, she gasped—an expression I recognized as the prelude to another scheme. She turned to me, her long lashes fluttering like bird wings, and I knew she wanted me to execute the plan. But I couldn't afford to get entangled in anything with Laura, of all people. Papa and Nana would have me kicked out of Richmond High and shipped off to boarding school—just as they had discussed a couple of years ago when Bianca's fat mouth blabbed that I had a crush on Laura.

Don't get me wrong. Papa and Nana accepted that I was gay—Papa just needed time to process it. They understood. Still, they despised Laura with a burning passion. It wasn't like I didn't get why. Laura had landed me in heaps of trouble back then—trespassing, stealing, vandalizing. Most of it was us getting even with Laura's dad for cheating on Mrs. Preston. Laura and I would follow his sluts, key their cars, or smash their windows. It was fun—exactly what Laura needed to cope. But my family wasn't having any of it. They insisted I end my friendship with her. For a while, I let them believe I had. Yet when the PLC came about, I saw it as my chance to prove Laura had changed. That is, until Phoebe entered the picture. Laura simply wouldn't let Phoebe off the hook.

"The game on Saturday night," Laura cried, her eyes wide. Even though I'd already collected the last shard, I continued inspecting her hand, eager to avoid her plan. "During our partner stunts—you could drop her." She withdrew her hand, envisioning the possibility. Lost in thought, she continued, "It would be so awesome. If she fell and broke something, it'd be the perfect way of getting her out—off the squad, the volleyball team, maybe even PLC." Her gaze locked with mine again. "I need you to do it."

"*Me*? I could get into serious trouble if I just dropped a girl on her head in front of hundreds of people."

"Well, it won't look that way. You can make it seem like an accident. Maybe even stumble yourself. No one will blame you for losing your footing."

"Laura, this has got to stop. How am I supposed to get away with this when everyone's watching?"

She shrugged. "Easily. You'll distract them with how sexy you are." A sly smile spread across her lips.

"Huh?" My heart picked up the pace. Blinking, she nodded matter-of-factly, then gingerly trailed a finger along my face. My shaking hands let the tweezers slip. I took a cautious step back. "What are you *doing*, Laura?"

She giggled. "Just relax. I won't bite. Well, maybe a little." Her eyes shone as if she were gazing at a million-dollar prize.

My insides turned to jelly as she inched forward, placing her arms on my shoulders. Her flowery perfume lingered in my nostrils. I struggled for balance, clutching her for support. But what was Laura doing so close? Was she about to kiss me?

My heart thumped wildly as her dark eyes focused on my lips. She leaned in, but I pulled away. "Are you okay with this?" I asked in a breathy tone.

Laura dropped her arms from my shoulders, and I almost slapped myself for ruining the moment. She glared at me, brows furrowing. "Why would you ask me that?"

I shrugged. "I don't know—because you're not gay?"

"How would you know?" She linked her pinkie finger with mine, staring at me with enormous doe eyes that dared me to kiss her. When I hesitated, she ran a couple of fingers down my back thigh, weakening my knees. I stumbled into her, practically melting into her soft body. Our eyes locked, and we shared a soft, tentative kiss. Laura's lips curled into a smile before pulling me closer for more. Her fingernails lightly raked my bare legs, sending goosebumps up my spine. When our tongues touched, I felt as if I might collapse into a ball of fluff. Laura guided me toward the bed, and we tumbled down, our hands entangled in each other's hair.

After a moment, we broke apart to catch our breath. I

lay there, struggling to process what had just happened. Laura *finally* realized how I felt, and she felt it too. I wanted to leap and turn a somersault. Instead, I grabbed her face and kissed her again.

Giggling, she pulled away, then straddled me. "Back to business. On Saturday, will you do it for me—drop Phoebe?" Laura whispered, pressing her mouth to my neck and suckling my flesh.

With a faint moan, I whipped my head back and said, "*Yes.*"

12

CASSIE

I SHOVELED ANOTHER BITE OF MA'S TABLE'S CHILI while perched on the ragged sofa in my dimly lit den. I should've been nearly blind from all those late-night homework sessions in that low light, but that was my only chance—during the six o'clock news before my shift at the diner.

I took another salty spoonful, grimacing as it slid down. The chili never lived up to the hype, but I couldn't afford to be choosy. With groceries never in stock at my place, a cup of chili was the only thing I could steal without my manager noticing—especially since we churned out pot after pot every day.

Flipping through my math book, I glanced at the

television.

"Local missing woman's family still pleading for answers."

I couldn't help but pout. Miss G was always there for me, knowing shit about me no one at Richmond High ever did. She had never once judged me; instead, she offered me advice. She even landed me the diner job thanks to her friendship with the owner. I hoped they'd resolve whatever was happening with her now. I missed Miss G like hell, but I couldn't pretend I didn't know why she'd disappear. If a sex video of me leaked, I'd vanish too. Hell, that's exactly what I'd do, if I were being honest. If Mom hadn't been transferred to Richmond Heights from her old job, I wouldn't have survived at my previous school.

The chili weighed in my stomach like lead, killing my appetite. I turned up the TV as baby Joey began fussing in his playpen in the corner. A tall, chubby guy was speaking about Miss G. With dark curly hair and a beard, he introduced himself as Charlie Samson—her fiancé. He didn't really seem like Miss G's type at all, but I guess the saying was true—opposites attract. I barely heard a word he said, since Mom burst through the back door ranting on her cell, as usual.

"You must think I'm a goddamn fool, don't you, Tony?" she barked, stepping into the doorway in a purple dress short enough to reveal her white panties. A lit cigarette dangled between the tips of her long, plastic fingernails. She looked tacky and cheap.

I turned away in disgust just in time to see Miss G's fiancé being consoled by who I assumed were her parents.

It was all so sad and heartbreaking. If Miss G didn't want to face the consequences, couldn't she have at least left a note assuring everyone she was okay? Would I have alerted someone if *I* were leaving? I caught a glimpse of Mom out of the corner of my eye.

"You can fuck whoever the hell you want. I've had my fun with you anyway. There's plenty of fish in the sea," she declared, hanging up the phone and pacing in front of the TV. "Fucking loser." She took a long drag.

God I wish I could leave now. Take Joey with me and go someplace fancy like the Sweet Haven—a luxury hotel with thick white robes and beds so big you could get lost in it.

The funky smell of cigarette smoke brought me back to reality.

"You can't smoke around the baby," I said.

She glared at me before blowing a puff of smoke in my direction. Still holding the cigarette in her lips, she thumbed through her cell and then made a call. "Johnny, hey?" she giggled. With a flirtatious toss of her long brunette curls over one shoulder, it was as if this Johnny guy could see her.

"Yes, it's me... Baby girl." She giggled some more. I rolled my eyes. She stepped toward the window, speaking so I couldn't hear her, but I knew she was looking to hook up.

I glared down at my trigonometry book, gritting my teeth. The numbers and symbols blurred together—my head swimming with Joey's cries, the pounding car ad on the TV, and Mom's excited whooping because her booty call had come through. I swallowed hard, ignoring the lump forming in my throat.

"Cassie? CASSIE?" Mom snapped those hideous nails at me. "What time are you leaving?"

"Soon. Why?"

"You need to shut that kid up and put him to bed before you go."

"Mom, please. I have to get this paper turned in

tomorrow. Can't you just…"

"I don't think so. I have my own life, you know?"

And by life, she meant hooking up with random men she met on MatchBox every other night.

"Jesus, Mom. You're home all day while *I'm* out trying to pay for this shit hole. The least you could do is watch Joey."

Her face twisted. "Just who the hell do you think you are to tell me what to do? *You're* the child."

"Then why are you behaving like one?" I gripped the edges of my book until the sharp corners dug into my palms.

"Hey, you don't get to judge me. The last I remember, you're no better than I am. What did they call you—*Cass-The-Quick-Piece-Of-Ass?*"

I slammed my trig book shut. "Stop it." I rose to my feet.

She laughed softly. "Shut that kid up and get him to bed. I don't need him disturbing my night." Fluffing her curls, she strutted out of the room.

With a sigh, I turned off the TV and dropped beside Joey's playpen.

"Hey there, little guy," I cooed, stroking his fine blond

hair. His wide dark eyes peered up at me as his bottom lip quivered for another sob. Gathering his bottle, I gently scooped him into my arms. "Don't you worry," I whispered. "I'm gonna get you out of here. That's a promise." I glanced toward the doorway to make sure Mom wasn't listening.

Once those college scouts recognized my talent, I'd snag a scholarship. Then, to hell with Mom's bullshit.

pHoeBe

On Saturday, the day of the big game, the cheerleaders were busy preparing in the locker room, chatting away. I sat on the edge of the bench, facing the lockers and distancing myself from everyone. I had nothing to say to anyone after what Zander had done. Without a cell signal, I had hiked nearly two miles that day before stumbling upon the nearest bus stop.

"Okay, gather around, ladies," Laura announced. Instantly, the locker room quieted as she strode to the center, her dark hair trailing behind her in her cheerleading uniform. "I know we're missing our cheerleading coach, but let's remember everything she taught us. We're going out there with our heads held high, ready to tear into those cats like the sharks we are!" The girls burst into cheers. "I have a few last-minute adjustments to make for the routine. Phoebe?"

I glanced up, surprised. "Yes?"

"I want you to be our flyer tonight."

Was she serious? "*Why?*"

"Excuse me?" Cassie pushed her way through the circle to face Laura. "*I'm* the flyer." Her usually innocent expression shifted to a frown, her blue eyes hardening.

Laura sighed. "Cass, I know—but Phoebe's stunts are sharper. We need to be as flashy as possible tonight."

"But *I'm* the best flyer, Laura," Cassie insisted.

I slowly rose from my seat. "Laura, she's right. Besides, I'm not up for a sudden change."

Laura spun to me, her dark eyes shimmering with intensity. "I cannot *believe* you two are arguing with me right now. I'm trying to put our best foot forward for Miss G," she said, her voice cracking as if she were about to cry.

"We don't have time to fight about it, guys," Mimi cut in. "Besides, Laura is the captain, and what she says goes." She scanned us all, a purple Tootsie Pop clutched in her hand.

"That's ridiculous. I'm so *sick* of Phoebe hogging all

the attention," Cassie snapped, jabbing a finger in my direction.

"*Cassie?*" I flinched.

"Fine. Whatever." Cassie threw up her hands and stormed out of the locker room.

Once she was gone, Laura released a long, heavy breath. "Well, that was interesting," she remarked, drawing a few chuckles from the others. I sank back onto the bench, feeling two feet tall. "You're good with it, right, B?" she asked me.

I struggled to answer when Zander suddenly barged into the locker room. My body froze—I hadn't seen him since that day.

Mimi quickly stepped in front of him. "This is the girls' locker room. Can't you read?"

"At the highest level, thank you very much," he replied smoothly. He hoisted Mimi off her feet and set her aside. "I came to see my favorite cheerleader, of course," he added, flashing that notoriously toothy grin.

He *couldn't* be ballsy enough to try something in front of the entire cheerleading squad. I shifted uncomfortably, my heart pounding, and focused on the floor until Laura let out an excited squeal as he scooped her up. Her legs wrapped around his waist, and he backed her against the lockers as they made out passionately, their moans and caresses filling the space.

"Alright, break it up!" Mimi clapped her hands, stepping between them. "If you don't get the hell out of here, Zander, I'm getting Principal McGee."

After giving Laura one more sloppy kiss, Zander let her feet touch the floor and shot me a glare as he headed for the door.

Laura, chest rising and falling, stared after him. "Well, that was even more interesting," she said. Everyone laughed at that, except for Mimi and me.

I was the last to leave the locker room a little while later. I couldn't shake the fury I'd seen in Cassie's eyes—though I understood it. Why would Laura change things at the last minute? With my head hanging low, I started for the gym.

In the hall, Ethan stood with his hands stuffed into his pockets. "I thought they locked you in a locker," he teased. I attempted a smile, though my lip was still sore and the cut inside my mouth hadn't healed. "You look beautiful," he said, gesturing at my uniform.

I rolled my eyes. "A dozen girls are wearing the same

outfit."

He studied me, as if trying to read my soul. I broke his gaze and looked down at the floor. "Do you want to talk?" he asked.

I shut my eyes for a moment, briefly reliving Zander's nightmare. I couldn't go down that road—not before the game. "No."

"Would you like a hug, then?"

I turned to him, scrunching my nose. He offered a lopsided grin and opened his arms. I managed a smile and gratefully stepped into his embrace, resting against his chest. As his heart thumped in my ear, I relaxed to its rhythm. Ethan's warm hold calmed me to the bone. After several seconds, he cleared his throat.

"If you don't get going, the Sharks will miss their best cheerleader."

Laughing, I broke away, but he caught me by the hand. "Will you find me when you're ready to talk?"

"Pinkie swear," I promised, wiggling my little finger.

"Clap your hands; it's time to shout!
Come on, fans; yell it out!
Say it loud; say it proud!

Let's go, Sharks, without a doubt!"

The Sharks finished the first half ahead, 45-43.

We ran through our cheer routine, parading and chanting, and the crowd was equally fired up. I even energized my performance for Rory, with Ethan right there in front of me, cheering me on.

As the other girls executed synchronized backflips on either side, Laura, Mimi, and Shayla gathered close as I launched into a back tuck into their waiting hands. Showing off a little flair, I balanced on one leg and raised my arms in a V shape. They dipped just as I spun into a 360-degree twist, with Mimi acting as my back spot. In the final moments before the catch, I caught a glimpse of Mimi faltering while Laura and Shayla reached for nothing.

Damn. I was plummeting straight to the floor!

With my eyes tightly shut, I braced for impact, only to feel strong hands shove against my back while Laura and Shayla grabbed my front.

"I've got you!" Cassie called.

Relief washed over me, and I longed to pull her into the tightest hug ever—Cassie had just saved my life.

When my feet finally met the ground, on impulse, the five of us struck synchronized poses to finish our routine. The crowd burst into applause and stomping cheers.

"Good job, ladies," Laura shouted over the clamor, smiling broadly at the audience.

"I can't thank you enough," I told Cassie after the game. The Sharks won: 69-53.

Flushing, Cassie shrugged. "It was teamwork."

"I don't understand how I tripped up," Mimi murmured, frowning at Laura, who was busy tongue-wrestling with Zander again. Mimi stalked over, clearly intent on breaking them up.

Gripping Cassie's arm, I said, "I'm sorry about the sudden change to the routine."

Cassie grinned. "It's cool—we killed it either way."

"That was *so* awesome, guys," Summer cried as she hurried over in her band uniform. She scooped up Cassie and me in a tight hug, her enthusiasm as over the top as ever.

Cassie stumbled but quickly regained balance.

"Alright—after-party time!" Laura called out. Zander stood behind her with an arm wrapped around her waist. I sensed his eyes on me, but I refused to meet his gaze.

"I have an idea," Summer said excitedly. Laura shot her a look that clearly asked why she was even here, but Summer pressed on, more bubbly than ever. "Why don't we set up camp tonight and go fishing in the morning? It'd be epic with the whole group—we could roast s'mores and hot dogs."

I mustered a weak smile while Zander and Laura laughed.

"Is she serious?" Zander said to Laura.

I clenched my fist, desperate to wipe the smirk off his face. "I think it's a great idea," I insisted.

Laura scoffed. "*I'm* not going fishing. That's what grocery stores are for. And by the way, I wasn't talking to you, *bandmate*—I meant the cheerleaders and, of course, the star of the show." Turning to Zander, their lips met again. "So, what do you all say?" she asked. "Pizza on me?"

"Sounds good," Cassie agreed.

Mimi nodded but kept shooting daggers at Zander. I wasn't in the mood to celebrate in his presence anyway—and if they didn't consider Summer an equal, I didn't care about pizza.

Laura led the way. "Let's go."

"I think I'll sit this one out," I said.

Laura whirled around, her temper flaring. "What? Because I don't want to watch her devour an entire pizza?" She shot a pointed look back at Summer, and Zander snickered.

"Laura, knock it off," I snapped. "She can hear you."

"My point exactly," Laura replied. "Why are you even here?" She turned to Summer, who was desperately fighting back tears.

I reached out to comfort Summer, but she pulled away and ran off. I glared at Laura. "Why do you always have to pick on her?"

Zander stepped in and draped an arm around Laura's shoulders. "She's just joking. *You* really shouldn't take everything so seriously." It was clear he was hinting at our incident, too.

"Look, I promise I'll apologize to her later," Laura said. "I'll even get her a gift. Now, will you come with us? Please?"

"No. I've got plans," I replied, scanning the stands until I spotted Ethan sitting alone in the front row. Our eyes met.

Laura sighed. "Phoebe, come *on*. It's our victory celebration. You really want to miss out?"

"Have fun, guys," I said as I headed toward Ethan. He gave me a small wave as I approached.

"Everything okay?" he asked, pushing his glasses up and rising to his feet.

"I need to get out of here. Can we go somewhere else?"

"You sure your friends won't be a problem?"

I glanced back at them. Zander's gaze was fixed on Ethan, his eyes filled with a menacing glare. "Let's go," I muttered, taking Ethan's hand.

———

"So," Ethan said, for what felt like the umpteenth time a half-hour later, as we strolled barefoot along the beach. A full moon hung low in the sky, making the waves shimmer like liquid silver. Still in my cheerleading uniform, I wrapped my arms around my waist; the cool, moist air by the shore enveloped us.

"Care to talk about the Shark's little squabble?"

I rolled my eyes. That was exactly what it was. "I guess you were right about my *friends*," I admitted, the word feeling less and less accurate.

I told him about how Laura behaved toward Summer.

"Maybe Laura is hurting too, and she's lashing out at others just to feel better about herself," he suggested.

"Even if that's the case, it doesn't excuse her actions," I replied.

"Of course, it doesn't. However, acknowledging or understanding Laura's situation might be a step toward a kinder Laura." He shrugged.

"What are you, a shrink?" I laughed, quickly regretting the jab as thoughts of Dr. Landry and my vandalized car swirled in my mind. Rich hadn't made a big deal once he found out the car was fixed—he was just relieved I hadn't been seriously hurt, though technically I had been, considering Zander's bullshit. But that was drama for another day.

"No—I learn by watching people," Ethan said. "So, is Laura really the reason you've been so down?"

My pace slowed. "No. That's another story…" I began.

He squeezed my hand. "You can tell me."

I took a deep breath and recounted everything—from the texts I'd accused Ethan of sending to the incident involving the raccoon and Zander.

Ethan's hand trembled as he dropped mine. "How come you never told me any of that?"

"So you can have an I-Told-You-So moment?" I said with a crooked smile, trying to hide my wounded feelings.

He clenched a fist, nibbling on his lip. "I could've kicked Zander right in his stupid face tonight."

Gently, I rested my hand on his shoulder. "Zander isn't worth any more of our time."

"But he can't just get away with that shit. Why haven't you told someone?"

"I don't know. That stuff he said about my character…" I murmured, casting my eyes away, realizing Ethan was clueless about Nichole's. Running a hand through my hair, I added, "Anyway, Zander's back with Laura. There's no way I'm going to expose him after that."

"I don't care about Laura. If Zander tries—"

"Nothing's going to happen, Ethan. I know now to avoid Zander at all costs. So—"

Ethan's eyes narrowed. "What if he tries something when I'm not there to protect you?"

"Did I hear that right…*protect me*?" I sputtered with a laugh.

He joined in. "I might not have Zander's muscles, but I know taekwondo." Striking a martial arts pose, he looked a bit silly, and I couldn't help but giggle. Then, to prove his point, Ethan jogged a few feet and executed a series of backflips.

My eyes went wide. "Whoa! Liam was right about you being acrobatic."

His expression soured. "Liam told you that?" he muttered, clenching his fist. "He's so stupid," he hissed under his breath.

But why was he so upset? Shifting his gaze toward the water, he fell silent, and I too got lost in the soothing rhythm of the waves.

"I was on the gymnastics team when I was a kid," he explained, glancing sidelong at me. "It embarrassed my dad—his only son flipping around with the girls instead of playing ball."

"Your dad sounds like a real insensitive jerk."

"Among other things," he grumbled, tucking his hands into his pockets.

I bumped his shoulder lightly. "At least you didn't turn out like him." He laughed sarcastically, and I stepped closer. "Really, your heart stretches from here to here," I said, tracing an invisible, wide heart across his chest with my finger.

His cheeks flushed. "That tickles."

Our smiles faded into a quiet understanding as we

gazed into each other's eyes. His warm, brown eyes shone under his glasses. I wrapped my arms around his waist and felt him lean in to plant a soft kiss on my forehead, drawing me into a heartfelt embrace.

As curfew loomed, we walked back to my car where my cellphone kept ringing.

I rolled my eyes. "That's probably my mom."

Ethan slid into the passenger seat. "Tonight was really…"

"Peaceful?" I finished, fumbling on the floor for my purse.

"Yeah. I'd love to do this again. It feels like when I'm with you, everything will be okay."

I paused. "Why do I feel the same way about you?"

He blew a playful raspberry. "You don't; you're just buttering me up."

He cracked more jokes, but my thoughts drifted. I always felt at peace with him—I could open up, be myself, and even cry if needed without fear of judgment. I dreaded my family, except for Rory. I struggled to find my place with Laura and the rest, and the guilt was unbearable whenever Summer came around. And then there's Zander…

I recalled Ethan's rose painting, that beautiful message—and my heart began to pound anxiously. While Ethan continued talking, I reached up, cupped his face, and kissed him. He returned the kiss, tender lips meeting mine in a sweet, innocent embrace. I climbed into his lap and ran my fingers through his hair, deepening our kiss despite the throbbing pain on my lip and the incessant ringing of my phone fading into the background. Ethan's steady breaths mixed with mine as I gripped his hair tighter, our passion growing, his hands settling by his sides while I moved mine onto his thighs. He gasped softly against my lips, and smiling, I kissed him even more.

After a moment of shared quiet, we paused to catch our breath, our foreheads gently touching.

Ethan's eyes, magnified behind his glasses, were wide and speechless. I played absentmindedly with a lock of his hair until he abruptly jerked, clearly reminded of something.

"What is it?" I asked, irritation creeping into my tone. "Damn, that phone." Still nestled in his lap, I rummaged in my purse and answered—it was Laura. What could she possibly want?

"Hello?"

"Phoebe! Where are you? I've been ringing your phone off the hook. They found Miss G."

A rush of air escaped my chest. "Well, that's just great. How is she? Where did she go?"

"She's dead, Phoebe."

13

SUMMER

I PULLED THE PAN OF SKINLESS CHICKEN THIGHS from the oven. They say it's healthier without the skin—as if *that's* where all the fat is stored.

If only it were that simple to extract the fat from my body, my life would be entirely different. I'd be pretty, accepted into Laura's circle, invited to after-parties, pool parties, and whatever other parties she had. Cute guys like Zander would ask me out on dates. *Kiss* me even.

The aroma of garlic and herbs nearly made me sick. I glared at the pan in disgust—not because the meat was slightly charred, but because I had trained myself to battle my cravings. If I could see every meal as nothing more than a plate of garbage, maybe I'd be able to control my portions and stick to a low-calorie diet. I've been trying forever to lose weight, and though I hadn't made any progress, I was convinced that with enough effort, it would eventually happen.

"Grandma, dinner's ready," I called, heading off to set the table. In the den, Grandma and our neighbor Grace sat watching the news, discussing Miss G's death yet again. Apparently, someone had strangled her and left her in her car, which was discovered just outside Richmond Heights. It was such a terrible tragedy.

I couldn't help but stew over how Miss G never picked me for the school auditions. She always made it clear that Phoebe was her favorite—and I understood why. Phoebe was thin, beautiful, popular, and could execute a back tuck flawlessly. I believed I could, too, if I practiced harder.

"It smells lovely in here, Summer," Grace said in a shaky voice as she entered the dining room. In my mind, it reeked of sewage, but I suppressed a laugh. Grace, with her slender frame and gray bobbed haircut, gave a startled cry as she took me in. "Why, look at you?" she exclaimed, her eyes landing on the Shark's cheerleading uniform I'd bought.

I flushed. "I practiced a while ago and didn't have time to change."

Grandma appeared in the doorway. "I told you, Grace—every day, this girl makes me so proud. That teacher they just found—you know, the one with that horrible story—she was the head of your group, wasn't she, Summer?" I nodded, forcing a smile. "Summer was her favorite," Grandma added. Grandma Lydia *never* knew when to stop talking.

I watched as she slowly made her way to her seat, looking like me in forty years—only shorter, stockier, with bouncy salt-and-pepper curls and chic cat-shaped glasses. Grandma Lydia had a blood clotting condition in her legs, so she relied on a cane, and she couldn't even drive for more than ten minutes at a time—not like we ever had a car. Still, we managed with the help of her senior assistance and my part-time job at the burger joint.

"Tell Grace about the Pink Ladies, Summer," Grandma urged, and Grace clapped giddily.

I gulped. "Let me grab dinner before it gets cold, then I'll share all the fun details." I slipped into the kitchen, my shoulders heavy with resignation. Grandma would be so disappointed if she knew I hadn't made the squad or the club—but I clung to hope. Now that Miss G was out of the picture, perhaps I could audition again once our new counselor and coach arrived. Maybe then even the less attractive girls would finally have a chance.

pHoeBe

After hearing about Miss G, I barely managed to get out of bed. The next day, the news stations covered the story, showing us the isolated wooded area where the car had been found. The realization of it was too much to bear. The swarm of police officers. The yellow crime tape. The ominous body bag. *Miss G's body.*

I had felt nauseous ever since, unable to face anyone, and even missed my first day at the art supply store, my new job.

I turned over on my damp pillow, trying to escape Mom's persistent knocking at the door.

"Honey, there's a boy here to see you. Can we come in?"

Ethan? I pushed myself up on one elbow, hastily sat upright, and ran my fingers through my frizzy hair. Pulling the blanket higher around my shoulders—I only wore a nightshirt—I managed a weak, "Come in."

Mom opened the door and ushered Ethan inside before giving me a curt smile and leaving, the door left ajar. Soon after, her bedroom door closed. Ethan lingered near the entrance, one hand in his pale blue hoodie pocket and the other clutching his backpack.

"You weren't returning my calls, so I brought your homework," he said, stepping closer. "How are you holding up?"

I shrugged. "And you?"

He shrugged in return, letting his bag slip to the floor as he sat beside me. His gaze drifted to the painting on the wall. "I'm just worried about you. Were you close to Miss G?"

I bit my lip and nodded. "She was my confidant," I murmured. "Who could do something so awful? Kill her and then just leave her there like that..." My voice broke.

Ethan wrapped an arm around me. "The police will catch the creep responsible," he assured, offering a sad smile as he brushed a stray strand of hair from my face. "Hey," he added, gently bumping his shoulder against mine. "I took the front door this time—no thorns." He lifted his posture in a playful manner that made me chuckle.

The blanket slipped from around my shoulders as he eased himself beneath, holding my hand. Our fingers intertwined, and both our hands landed on my bare thigh. Ethan licked his lips nervously. "Um, about Saturday night... Is now a bad time to talk about it?"

I shook my head.

"Well, I've been thinking about it—a lot," he admitted. "Wondering what happens next, what it all meant. Should I back off if it was just a hookup?"

I cupped his chin, turned him to face me, and pressed my lips to his. Even after I pulled away, his eyes stayed shut. I smiled, giving him a quick peck on the nose. He opened one eye and giggled, and I snuggled into his arm, resting my head against his chest.

"Let's not overthink it. Whatever happens, will happen, okay?" I whispered, glancing up at him. He nodded, a satisfied smile on his face.

Ethan stayed over that day. Mom was working the night shift, but Rich was home, keeping out of our way. Ethan and I made homemade macaroni and cheese, using a recipe we found on Google with ingredients from my fridge. When it was ready, we sat on the floor in the den, surrounded by our schoolbooks with the TV on.

When the six o'clock news came on, it was about Miss G. Somehow, the authorities had discovered the video and considered it a break in her case.

I turned to Ethan, a spoonful of pasta going down the wrong pipe. "Do you think…?" My chest ached.

Rich cleared his throat, announcing his presence. "Someone is going to speak to you about that video first thing in the morning. Didn't you record it?"

My breaths were sharp. I nodded, chewing gingerly on my lip.

Ethan spoke up before I could. "But she isn't in trouble or anything, is she?

"No, of course not. We just have to follow up on all of Giselle's whereabouts leading to her murder. Don't worry, Phoebe. I'll be there with you."

I stared at Ethan once Rich left. "I really fucked up, didn't I?"

***

Two detectives came to speak with me bright and early the next morning. I hadn't even got dressed for school yet. They asked how I got the video and why I shared it online. I explained the Loony Saloon business and sneaking to see

Liam perform. I admitted to sharing the video *only* with Laura and them just for laughs. I had no part in what happened after. But no matter how I tried to steer away from the scandal, none of it would've happened if not for me. What if the detectives thought that video had something to do with Miss G's murder? If so, didn't that make *me* responsible?

When I got to school that day, I discovered somebody else had already passed that judgment on me. In bold, drippy black letters, they'd spray painted KILLER on my locker door.

14

pHoeBe

"COME OUT OF THERE, PHOEBE," RORY CALLED through the door that night.

How could anyone assume I was involved in Miss G's death? I had no motive. The only thing I did was record that video as proof I saw the teachers together. I was guilty of being a dumbass, not of *murder*.

Rory called again. "Listen, you did record that video, but you didn't physically murder anyone, nor did you order a killing. If you want to wallow in self-pity over something some asshole spray-painted, then fine."

I gasped and sat up straight. What if Zander was the one who spray-painted that message on my locker? He was the biggest asshole I knew—and I was almost in tears over what he thought?

At a quarter to eleven, Mom knocked on my bedroom door and stepped in. "Phoebe, I just wanted to let you know that if you ever need to talk..."

"I'm fine," I mumbled, staring at the ceiling.

"I know you say that, but Rich and I are here for you. And Dr. Landry is—"

"Mom, please don't," I managed to choke out, biting my lip. The last thing I needed was them worrying that I needed medication again. I exhaled shakily and leaned back against the headboard.

Mom sat on the edge of my bed. "If you're up for it, I'd like to show you some pictures."

Pictures of what? She pulled out a worn, tattered photo album. The first page held a picture of her and Dad—only a few years older than me. Dad even had the charm of a young John Stamos, and Mom looked beautiful with her blonde curls and doe-like eyes.

"This was taken on our first date," she explained. "Your father took me to the movies. He was so nervous he ended up spilling his milkshake all over himself."

She flipped the page to reveal a photo of her with Rich,

seemingly from the same year. I rolled my eyes at Rich's mullet, then blinked in surprise—there they were, holding hands. I looked at her, silently pleading for an explanation.

"Your father and Rich were college roommates. I dated Rich several months before I met your dad. It was Rich who introduced us. He was just your average Joe, but your dad was everything—charming, charismatic, sexy." She nudged me playfully. "You could even say he stole me away from Rich."

We laughed together, and after a moment, Mom sighed. "But somewhere along the line, he lost his way. Believe me, I wished I could have done something, but it was too late by then. In his suicide note..."

I caught my breath. "He left a note?"

She nodded. "In time, I'll let you read it."

"Promise?"

"Of course, sweetheart." She gently tucked a stray lock of hair behind my ear. "In that note, he asked Rich to take care of us. Apparently, he was the only man David ever trusted with his family." I stared at the photo of Mom and Rich, utterly confused.

"You should get some sleep," she said, easing to the

edge of the bed, but I stopped her.

"Do you think Dad would be proud of me, who I am today?"

"Absolutely, Phoebe. I know that because *I* am." I grabbed her and hugged her tight. When we pulled away, she grinned. "So, that Ethan…? Is he your boyfriend?"

My face warmed. "We're…figuring it out."

"Well, I'm happy for you. Ethan is such a gentleman—and really cute, too." Her eyes widened.

"*Mom.*"

LAURA

I paced in my bedroom, fists clenched, as my stupid parents screamed at each other downstairs. I *wasn't* going to Rome with my dad and he didn't have the balls to come up and tell me. The lousy son of a bitch didn't *want* me to go with him.

"What is the *matter* with you, Jack?" Mom demanded, her voice tight.

Her words bewildered Dad. "*Me? You* imposed on my plans. Laura was never supposed to be invited. You're trying to dump her off on me because *you* don't even want her around. Look, I can't stay and talk, Beth. Angela's out there waiting for me."

Of course, that bitch was. Angela was Dad's twenty-something gold digger girlfriend. I couldn't even hate on her, though. If Dad was dumb enough to give Angela the world and then some, why *not* accept it? But damn. He thought that bitch was more important than me?

"Get back here, Jack," Mom barked, followed by shuffling as they approached the hall. "I'm damned if I'm going to do your dirty work. Tell Laura you're not taking her with you. Jack—go tell her! Jack!" And then the front door slammed.

I approached the window and saw Dad hurrying off to his Lincoln, with Angela patiently waiting in the passenger seat. I pressed my lips together and swallowed my hurt. Fuck Dad and fuck Rome. I didn't need either of them. Zander was back in my life, and that was all that mattered.

I grabbed my cell phone to call him, only to find dozens of missed calls and texts from Mimi. What the hell did that clingy bitch want? As I swiped away her notifications, she called again. "What?" I answered.

"*What?*" Mimi repeated, laughing nervously. "I was

just wondering what you were doing tonight. Can I come over?"

"You can't. Zander's here, and I'm about to rock his world," I whispered into the phone, a devious smile spreading across my lips. I was definitely *hoping* to.

Mimi was quiet a beat. "Are you serious, Laura? What about us?"

Us? Was she *crazy*? "Sorry, Mimi, but I gotta go." I blew a kiss and hung up. There was no way in hell *we* would ever be an item. Besides. Damn her for even implying I'd give up Zander. Mimi knew exactly how much he meant to me—she was supposed to be my best friend. How dare she force me to choose?

I scrolled to Zander's contact with a sour taste lingering in my mouth. *Fuck* Mimi, too.

On the fifth goddamn ring, Zander finally answered. "Hey, you?"

What the hell was taking him so long? Rolling my eyes, I flipped my hair and turned on the charm. "Wanna hook up tonight?" I purred sultrily. After a pause, my smile vanished.

"Uh…" he drawled clearly weighing his words. "I'm with a few of the guys. Let me call you, say, in an hour?"

He hung up before I could reply.

In frustration, I flung the phone against the wall. That son of a bitch was distant again. Was Phoebe still the reason? Was posting that video not enough reason to turn on her? Phoebe was far from perfect. How could I make him see that? *Damn*.

Glancing at my own frowning reflection, I realized I could use Mimi's company after all—I needed her *assistance*. I calmly collected the pieces of my shattered cell phone, reassembled it, and dialed Mimi back, and she answered immediately.

"H-hello?"

Was she *crying*? That pathetic bitch. "Hey. Change of plans. Still want to drop by?"

She sniffed. "Of *course*. I'll be right there."

I hung up and whirled around to see Mom standing in the doorway. I jumped in surprise. "Can't you knock?"

She rolled her eyes. "There are two detectives downstairs looking for you. What did you do this time?"

I smirked at her sarcasm. But seriously. What *did* detectives want with me?

15

pHoeBe

"PHOEBE, IT IS SO NICE TO MEET YOU," MRS. WHITE declared. She rose from behind Miss G's desk and shook my hand. The lingering scent of lemon still filled the room. Mrs. White, the new counselor, cheerleading coach, and head of the PLC, exuded confidence.

I already knew they'd eventually replace Miss G. That thought felt like a betrayal—and I quickly withdrew my hand, taking a seat. My eyes were drawn to a large gold envelope on the desk bearing the name PHOEBE HALL.

"How are you?" she asked. Mrs. White was heavyset, with flowing raven curls and ice-blue eyes visible behind thick-framed glasses. She rested a hand on my folder and continued before I could reply. "It says here you attempted suicide after your father died."

What a way to start the day.

"It appears you were close to Giselle Fischer. She had nothing but praise for you in her notes—she talked about all your improvements."

I barely managed a word as the meeting dragged on, with Mrs. White treating my file as if I were some case study. I simply nodded through her ten-minute monologue, listening to facts I already knew. When Mrs. White finally finished, she reassured me I could come talk to her anytime. She had no idea my faith in her had already flown out the window.

My day *had* gotten off to a positive start, though. Everyone—Mom, Rich, Rory, and I—had breakfast together. Rich cooked eggs Florentine, with freshly squeezed orange juice. Although Rich knew about Miss G's case, he didn't discuss any of it with me. Rory insisted he walk me to my locker to ensure there wasn't any funny business, and there wasn't. People were still whispering when I passed, but no one said anything directly to me. At lunch, I sat with Summer and Ethan. I wasn't ready to hear any of Laura's theories about Miss G's death, and I was still mad at her for how she'd treated Summer on the night of the game.

Summer was animatedly discussing the fishing trip the three of us planned to take that weekend when Laura approached our table. She placed a thin box in front of Summer. It was from Nichole's.

"For me?" Summer asked, blinking at Laura eagerly.

I did, too, eyeing Laura as if to say, *that's all?*

Laura cleared her throat. "Summer, I sincerely apologize to you for my negative comment," she said, staring Summer right in the eyes. "It was totally out of line, and I'm deeply sorry."

Summer's cheeks colored. "You're already forgiven."

Laura gripped Summer's shoulder. "Well, go on. Open it."

Summer bounced in her seat, excitedly lifting the top. It was a silver chunky bracelet with a heart pendant. "I love it so much."

With a curt nod, Laura strolled back to the cheerleader's table, where the rest of the gang watched everything. After a beat, they went back to chattering.

Summer gasped suddenly. "I should've invited her to go fishing with us." She stood, but I grabbed her arm.

"Summer, let's just stick to our plans for now," I said. "You can invite Laura next time."

She thought about it, slowly lowering into her seat. "Well, I guess so."

During cheerleading practice that afternoon, Mrs. White announced, "I am very honored to be with such beautiful, talented ladies," before her eyes landed on me. "Phoebe, I understand you're the captain?"

Laura immediately stepped forward with a frown. "That would be me. And she's the co-captain," she declared, pointing at Mimi, who was nonchalantly eating a chocolate Tootsie Pop.

Mrs. White chuckled nervously. "My apologies—I've lost my notes. Give me just a moment," she said, retreating to the bleachers to sift through her tote.

Laura spun on her heel and rolled her eyes. "She needs to coach track and lose some weight," she whispered. A few girls snickered. Sensing my hesitation, Laura quickly added defensively, "That was for Miss G."

I couldn't help but smile and shake my head at her comment.

Despite the earlier mix-up, practice went well. Mrs.

White quickly adapted, identifying our strengths and weaknesses with ease. She emphasized the need for balance as we prepared for the upcoming cheerleading camp in a few weeks, and we together committed to giving it our all in honor of Miss G.

After practice, I took a long, hot shower. By the time I stepped out, the room was empty and filled with a pleasant warmth, the steam lingering like a soft fog. Wearing only a towel, I padded through the haze toward the bench where I'd left my clothes—only to find that everything was gone. Even my uniform had vanished.

Puzzled, I prodded the steamy floor with my toe, searching for any sign of my belongings. Clutching the towel tighter, I headed for the locker room, hoping someone had put my things away.

I grabbed the door handle and turned, but the door remained firmly shut. Tugging it harder, I grunted—was it locked? I slapped my palm against the wood. "Anyone there?" I called, pulling and tugging, yet the door wouldn't budge. "Hey! I'm trapped in here!" I spun around frantically, checking the bench for my cell phone, but it was nowhere to be found. I was certain I had left my things there—like always. What the hell happened?

Heat pooled in my chest as I stumbled back to the door and tried again, louder this time. Still nothing. With an exasperated sigh, I pressed my forehead against the door, one hand on the handle and the towel clutched in the other. Eventually, I sank onto the empty bench and scanned the room—no windows, no vents. I was trapped.

Eyes blurred, I bit my lip and forced calm. Someone would notice if I failed to show up for Rich's Salisbury steaks dinner; he had everyone promise to come home together. Practice ended at four, and dinner was usually at six-thirty or seven. No way I could wait *that* long.

I sprawled on the floor in search of my cell phone, hoping it had slipped beneath the bench. In desperation, I looked everywhere, but nothing turned up. Just as I climbed to my feet in resignation, the door clicked and slowly swung open. I froze, towel clutched to my body. Cool air immediately replaced the hot steam, sending shivers down my legs. "Hello?"

Mr. Diggs appeared, clutching a mop. "I'm not dressed, Mr. Diggs," I shouted in relief that he had opened the door.

"Huh?" he sputtered, turning away as he hurried to shut the door.

"No—wait! I need to use the locker room." I tripped over my feet as I lunged to keep the door from closing. I was so happy to be free I nearly forgot I was wearing nothing but a towel. Mr. Diggs, with his back turned, hobbled toward the exit just as Laura walked in.

"Phoebe, what are you…?" she began, glancing between me and Mr. Diggs as he brushed past on his way out. "Why the hell was he down here while you were showering? Was he watching you?" Her voice rose. She spun on her heel and stormed off.

"Laura, wait," I called after her, cursing under my breath. I turned toward my locker and there, to my amazement, were my clothes neatly folded on the bench. I quickly pulled them on and rushed to intercept the unfolding drama. My chest pounding, I stopped at the end of the hall where I heard Laura inside Principal McGee's office, angry as she ranted about Mr. Diggs.

"Phoebe?" Principal McGee asked as I entered.

I raised my hands. "Sir, there's been a misunderstanding."

"Misunderstanding, Phoebe?" Laura snapped, turning on me. "That guy is obsessed with you—it's sick."

"Laura, *stop*," I growled through clenched teeth.

"Principal McGee, I got locked in the shower stall. Mr. Diggs had no idea I was down there—he actually helped me." I glared at Laura.

"And the texts? You still don't believe it was Diggs?" she countered.

"What texts?" Principal McGee interjected. As Laura and I exchanged steely glares, he stepped between us. "Both of you need to go home. I will speak to Mr. Diggs. Now, go."

My lips pressed together as I trailed after Laura outside before I could say more. "Why did you do that, Laura? You don't even know what really happened."

"Why are you defending him, Phoebe? Don't tell me you like that creep's attention?" she spat, disgust etched in her tone.

"But you're wrong! He didn't do anything—Diggs didn't text me either. It was all Zander." I blurted out without regret.

Laura stepped back, appalled. "What?"

"It was Zander. He admitted everything after I pieced it together."

Laura's face twisted in anger with each word. "You are such a conceited bitch, Phoebe."

"Laura, it's the truth. Just ask him."

Laura strolled off, taking the stairs two at a time. Her ponytailed hair swung angrily with each stride. "Phoebe says you sent her threatening texts?" she declared, stopping in front of Zander, her eyes narrowing suspiciously.

Zander laughed derisively. "Threatening texts? What on earth are you talking about?" He glanced over Laura's shoulder at me. "Why would I do that?"

My mouth went dry. "Zander, tell the truth. You left a dead raccoon in my car. You slashed my tires." Laura looked back and forth between me and Zander, confusion spreading across her face.

Zander touched her arm. "Babe, I have no idea what she's talking about. All I know is that after our first date or whatever, I had to turn her down. She isn't what I thought. I mean, what happened at Nichole's—with her exposing her teachers…"

I couldn't believe what I was hearing. "*Tell* her about the burner phone, Zander."

He kept his eyes fixed on Laura. "I realized I wasn't over you, after all. When I told Phoebe that, she still tried to kiss me. She went wild—attacking me and screaming."

"He's lying!" I burst out, angry tears blurring my vision. "*He* forced a kiss on *me*."

Laura gasped and spun towards me, but Zander quickly turned Laura's face toward his. "Babe, I'm sorry we ever even broke up." Instantly, Laura's smile softened into something sweet, yet she quickly glared at me as if I were filth.

"Laura, please believe me," I pleaded, reaching out, but she slapped my hand away.

"Go to hell, Phoebe."

"But you can't believe a word Zander says!" Before I could react further, Ethan's grip came up on me.

"Come on, Phoebe. Let's go." He led me toward my car.

"That bastard just lied in front of everyone."

"Well, what did you expect him to do, Phoebe—the right thing? Zander will do whatever it takes to save himself. I warned you what kind of person he was."

I pounded the roof of the car in frustration. "I wish I could've punched him in his stupid face."

"Do you believe in karma?" Ethan asked calmly.

"I don't know. Why?"

He didn't reply.

16

pHoeBe

"JUST TAKE YOUR TIME," DR. LANDRY SAID ON Friday, his tone half-annoying, half-soothing.

I shut my eyes and exhaled slowly. "I saw him again." It hurt to admit it. My eyes flicked to Dr. Landry's, waiting for his reaction, but he just nodded silently, urging me to continue. After a hoarse cough, I went on, "I was at work. A customer needed help finding the fan brushes. You know, the ones for blending paint?" Of course, he didn't know—they were for an artist, not a doctor.

"Anyway, when I got to the paintbrush aisle, the guy was rummaging through various brushes, his back turned to me. There was something about his build—the broadness of his shoulders, his dark hair resting just above his collar, just like..." I lowered my eyes as embarrassment washed over me. What happened next was insane.

"Phoebe?" Dr. Landry called.

Tilting my head and gazing at the fig plant in the corner, I answered, "I rushed up to the guy and wrapped him in a huge embrace. I held him tight, telling him how much I missed him." My vision clouded with tears, though I refused to let any fall. I laughed instead. "That poor man was so confused. And of course, when he turned, he looked nothing like him. Not even close."

I forced another laugh, and Dr. Landry smiled at me sympathetically. I knew that smile all too well—he was about to put me back on medication. I clenched my fists, letting my nails dig into my wet palms. The word "mistake" danced around in my head, and I muttered it aloud.

Dr. Landry squinted behind his glasses. "What's that?"

"I made an honest mistake, Dr. Landry. I know with one-hundred percent certainty that my dad is gone and that no matter how closely someone might resemble him, it's not him."

He nodded in satisfaction, and I took that as a good sign—until, moments later, he slid a prescription slip across the table. The bomb of anxiety exploded in my stomach. I blinked at him, trembling. "What is that?"

"It's only a mild sedative to help calm you when you're feeling anxious."

I shook my head slowly and looked back at the fig plant, my eyes watery as I dabbed at them with my fingers. Dr. Landry's arm remained extended across the table as he tapped the slip. "Phoebe? Look at me. This isn't a step backward. When you lead a busy life, it's hard to relax. How are you liking the new job so far? Despite that slight confusion."

That situation was far from minor, though I appreciated that he was trying to keep things light—to let me know he didn't think I was crazy.

Just an hour earlier, an older woman had screamed at me for overcharging her for her grandkid's coloring pencils. The drama at school had distracted me from concentrating lately.

Principal McGee had investigated Mr. Diggs further— by questioning other girls like Mimi, Cassie, and several from the cheerleading team—who all confirmed that Mr. Diggs was a peeping Tom. That was all Principal McGee needed to hear. They fired Diggs before he could even blink.

Then, authorities saw Liam as a person of interest in Miss G's case. The two had hooked up several times before I caught them together. The rumor was that he was upset Miss G wasn't leaving her fiancé.

Miss G's family held a private ceremony. Only immediate family attended the funeral, but, like Coach Thorne, Richmond High held a candlelit vigil for her.

Ever since Zander's confrontation, Laura had done her best to avoid me. She wouldn't talk to me at practice, and when the PLC got together yesterday to deliver groceries to the elderly, she wouldn't even look at me—even though we were partners.

If I could, I would drop out of school again, but I knew Mom and Rich wouldn't let that happen. Besides, I needed everyone to believe I wasn't spiraling back into the rabbit hole.

I straightened in my seat and forced a smile. "It's going okay. Time just flies by."

"Are you meeting new people?" he asked while

scribbling on his pad.

"No, but I do engage in small talk with everyone," I shrugged. "Should I be meeting new people?"

He shook his head. "I'm sure you're adapting just fine." Sliding his glasses up on his nose, he asked, "How are things looking at home?"

"Better. I'm finally accepting Rich for who he is. My relationship with Mom has strengthened, too. She even trusts me with a little more freedom."

Except now, I wasn't close to anyone anymore. There was no way Laura was inviting me over for sleepovers again. Speaking of which, I glanced at the clock—I was supposed to meet Summer and Ethan soon to go fishing. I wanted to cancel, but I refused to bail on Summer. She'd been looking forward to it as if it were Christmas.

"Okay. That's a huge improvement. But any particular reason all of that happened?"

I didn't have time to explain. I was already running late. Checking the clock once more, I licked my lips nervously. "Um, just a change of heart, I guess. Everyone wants a happy home. Plus, Rich isn't as bad as I thought, and he makes Mom happy—so he's worth a chance." I must have earned some brownie points for that because he then wrote something else with a wide grin on his face.

"Excellent, Phoebe. I'm so very proud of you. Just remember, no one is perfect. Our sessions aren't about turning you into a flawless being—it's about guiding you toward the best version of yourself. There's nothing wrong with getting help or support from those you love." He gestured toward the prescription slip again. "I'd like you to take one of these pills tonight before bed, and going forward, only when you're feeling anxious, okay?" His pleading eyes made it almost seem like he knew I wouldn't take it.

———

A short while later, Mom glanced up from the table as I entered through the back door. She was flipping through a magazine while a kettle warmed on the stove. "Hey, honey. How'd it go? Anything… new?" she asked, raising a brow.

"Nope," I replied, shaking my head as I popped my P. "Dr. Landry says I'm the best I've ever been." The memory of Summer's over-the-top attitude flashed through my mind as I tried to muster a wide smile. "I even *feel* my best."

I needed Mom to believe me. If she knew Dr. Landry

had prescribed a new sedative—even a mild one—she'd never let me see the light of day again. She'd restrict me from all the sharp objects and make me pee with the door open. I wasn't sure she'd go *that* far, but I certainly wouldn't have any privacy.

Eyes lighting up, Mom placed both hands flat on the table, her mouth open in astonishment. "Phoebe, I'm so glad to hear that. You're handling things so well."

But she didn't know about my recent incident, so I savored her compliments. I might have even done a backflip—if not for the kettle whistling and interrupting her.

"Hey, I'm making this instant chai tea latte. Do you want some?" she asked, rising to get the kettle.

My body tensed as she passed by, and I grew paranoid she might hear the pills in my purse clinking as if they were alive. "Um, no, I don't think I have the time, *but* I'll take a rain check."

She turned to me, beaming as she clutched a small packet. "Well then, go catch us some dinner."

—————

I rolled to a stop in front of Summer's home—a small, rundown antebellum-style house with a crooked porch and two rocking chairs that exuded a bit of southern charm. An older, heavy-set woman eyed my approach from behind glasses perched on the tip of her nose. "Summer, the girls are here!" she yelled toward the house. Waving, the woman stood and hobbled down the stairs, leaning on a cane for support.

I waved back from the passenger window. "Hi there."

"You must be Phoebe," she said as she leaned through the window with her palm outstretched. "All Summer ever talks about is *Phoebe this or Phoebe that*." My cheeks burned as I shook her hand. Noticing, she added, "I'm sorry to put you on the spot, dear. I'm just grateful Summer's hard work paid off. She has no idea how proud I am that she's part of that pink club and the cheerleading squad." With a little wiggle, she asked, "Say, where *are* the other young ladies, anyway?" Her eyes darted around my empty car.

I sat there, stoned-faced and completely lost for words. "Um, they're already… there…" It came out like a question.

"Grandma! What are you doing?" Summer snapped from behind her.

The woman straightened with a cheerful chuckle. "Just

being polite, dear. Don't throw a hissy fit!" She wagged a finger playfully at Summer, who was clearly annoyed.

I'd never seen her angry before. Her face had flushed completely.

"*Go take your nap*," Summer ordered through clenched teeth.

Her grandmother protested for a moment before relenting. "Alright, you girls have fun, okay? And remember," she said to Summer, "put extra meaning into your rah-rahs, okay, dear? I'll wait up for you, Sum," she added, heading back into the house.

With an exasperated sigh, Summer climbed into the passenger seat. As if someone had pressed a start button, she instantly returned to her perky self. "Chello!" she spun to me and giggled.

My lips tightened as I struggled to smile back. What was going on? Why did her grandmother think she was a cheerleader?

"Please excuse my grandma," she said. "My parents are away on a business trip, so I'm staying with her for a little while. She means well, but she can be a bit…" She twirled at her temple. "Usually, she's at her bingo game. I don't know why she stuck around." Nodding, I started the car.

"What was she saying to you?"

"Huh?" I licked my lips. "Oh, nothing. Just introducing herself."

Summer clamped her hand on my shoulder and leaned close to peer into my face. "That's all?"

After glancing at her grip, I focused on the windshield and put the car in reverse. "Yep. Nothing else."

17

pHoeBe

Despite the awkward moment at her place, I still had a great time with Summer. Shortly after, I picked up Ethan, and just as Summer promised, she took us to a stream where we spent nearly two hours catching salmon. The soothing water and lush green scenery made it incredibly relaxing—I hadn't realized how much I'd come to appreciate nature. I caught one fish, Ethan got zip, and Summer, the expert, snagged three. She insisted Ethan and I take them since her grandmother had already prepared a pot of gumbo for dinner.

Later, Mom invited Ethan over for dinner. He arrived bearing flowers for her and a store-bought chocolate cake for dessert. Ethan quickly became the highlight of the evening, laughing at Rich's lame jokes and praising Mom for her cooking. Everyone adored him—except Rory, who thought Ethan was a corny suck-up and couldn't resist making a wisecrack after every sentence.

I missed Ethan on Sunday because Mom insisted the family go to church—something we hadn't done since I was little. Then, when I spotted him on Monday after second period, I rushed over and planted a sloppy kiss on him; I was just that excited. After a few seconds of confusion, he wrapped his arms around me and kissed me back, only to take a sharp breath when we pulled apart

"What was *that* for?" he asked.

I tugged at his mohawk. "For being the best boyfriend ever and putting on that charming act for my family."

He rolled his eyes playfully. "Aren't I charming always?"

Giggling, I leaned in to kiss him again, but he pulled away. "You know people are staring, right?"

I tossed my hair over my shoulder. "So what?"

"So… are we making it official for everyone that we're an item?"

I stepped back, raising an eyebrow. "Do you not want

people to know you're taken?"

"Don't be ridiculous."

Smiling, I took his hands. "In that case, let's give them something to look at." I leaned in for a slow, passionate kiss. His cheeks flushed as we broke apart. "See you after practice?"

He glanced away nervously. "Sure. Actually, there's something I've been meaning to talk to you about."

"Okay. Anything I should be concerned about?"

The bell rang, and relief washed over his face. "I'll meet you by the bike station, okay? I gotta run." After giving me a quick peck on the cheek, he jogged off to class. Baffled, I watched him disappear and then spotted Zander glaring at me from the end of the hall.

"Come *on*, girls. Are we really going to take that low energy to camp? Pump it up!" Mimi shouted as she marched ahead of us—noticeably without her usual Tootsie Pop.

We had cheerleading practice on the lawn while the basketball team practiced in the gym. It was the hottest day of the week, a scorching eighty-five degrees, and the sun beat down so fiercely our shirts clung to our backs.

Everyone was irritated and thirsty, desperate for the practice to be over.

I bent forward, resting both hands on my knees.

"Something the matter, B?" Mimi asked.

Squinting against the sweat dripping into my eyes, I exhaled in exasperation. "I need a break, Mimi—I think we all do." I straightened up and wiped my eyes with the end of my shirt. Suddenly, nausea hit me—I wasn't sure if it was from flipping too much in the heat or the green bean casserole at lunch not agreeing with me. It could have been both. I just knew that if Mimi didn't ease off, she'd end up getting barfed on.

Some of the other girls slowed too, clearly exhausted.

"Here," Laura called, tossing me a bottle of Gatorade. I caught it quickly.

"Thanks," I sputtered, fumbling with the cap and surprised she even spoke to me. As I shakily brought the bottle to my lips, Laura leaned in to whisper something to Mimi.

Mimi rolled her eyes. "Well, since you're all chickening out, I guess we could call it a day."

"Where's Mrs. White, anyway?" Cassie asked, dabbing her forehead with the back of her hand.

"She had a family emergency," Laura explained. "Alright, ladies—I'm with Mimi now. Tomorrow, I want our energy levels through the roof. You sounded like zombie cheerleaders today." She even mimicked our tired tone.

I nearly spritzed my drink laughing. We really *did* sound like zombies. "Once we're out of this heat, I'm sure we'll bounce back," I said.

Laura turned her nose up at me. "I sure hope so. Don't embarrass me in front of the other cheerleading captains. Anyway, that's it for the day. Go on." With a dismissive wave of her hands, she sent us on our way.

I spun on one heel, feeling a little better already.

Cassie fell into step beside me, her straight blond hair pulled back in a fishtail braid that she tugged at nervously. "Is Laura still mad at you?"

"No," I played dumb. "Why? Has she said something about me?"

Cassie shrugged. "Nah, it just seems like there's some tension between you two—and you don't seem like her favorite anymore."

"Oh, not that again," I grumbled as I took another sip from my bottle, trying to wash away the sour taste.

"I'm kidding," Cassie said, bumping shoulders with me.

Just as we reached the doors, Liam burst from the school, clutching a box of his belongings.

"Li—I mean, Mr. Little! Hi," I called.

He blinked at me, as if trying to recall my name.

Cassie grabbed my arm. "We have to get going," she whispered, pulling me toward the exit. But I loosened my grip to watch Liam, noticing the dark rings under his eyes. A pang of grief hit me—I owed him an apology.

"Phoebe," he said kindly, offering a polite smile while reaching into his box. He pulled out a rolled-up painting and handed it to me.

It was my eye painting.

"Mr. Little, what's going on?" My heart pounded, though I quickly figured it out—they fired him.

"Phoebe, we have to go," Cassie insisted, louder now as she tugged my arm again.

Liam mumbled something like "*take care, ladies*," but I couldn't catch it as the doors closed behind us.

"What the hell is your problem?" I demanded.

"Why are you talking to him? He's a *murderer*."

I rolled my eyes. "Cassie, you shouldn't believe

everything you hear. Don't you think that if he were a murderer, he'd be behind bars by now?"

"Have you not been following his story? I'm not just talking about Miss G. Look at this."

I followed her to her locker, where she pulled out her phone, tapped a few times, then held it up to show me a Twitter post that read:

Liam Little's sister is a murderer and so is he!
#justice4MissG #lockhimup #guilty

Below the tweet was a link to a newspaper article about Ethan's parents—the headline in bold letters.

WOMAN PLED GUILTY TO HUSBAND'S MURDER

"Do you think she's Ethan's *mom*?" Cassie asked with a nervous giggle.

"Put it away," I snapped.

"But I haven't even shown you the—"

"I don't care!" I shoved her hand when she tried to show me more. "None of that proves Liam killed Miss G." My heart pounded—where was Ethan? I couldn't imagine what he must be feeling if the rumor mill was churning out stuff about his mom.

"I guess you and Ethan *have* gotten pretty serious," Cassie grumbled, slipping her phone back into her locker. "Just be careful, okay?"

"Nobody knows anything for sure, Cass."

She closed her locker and gripped my shoulder. "Be. Careful."

I eventually met Ethan at the bike station as planned, but he seemed in a hurry—struggling with his bike's lock, as if he were leaving without talking.

"Hey, Ethan!" I called, waving as he briefly looked my way before rushing back to his lock. As I approached, he tried to put on his helmet, but I caught his hand. "Are you okay?"

He pried my hand away. "I have to get home. They fired Liam."

I brushed my damp hair behind my ears. "Yeah, I kinda wanted to talk to you about that." Ethan shifted, turning so I couldn't see his face. I frowned. "Are you mad at me?" I grabbed his shoulder and spun him around. My chin nearly bumped my chest—he had a swollen eye and a split lip with drying blood. "What happened to you?"

He fiddled with the handlebars. "I can't find my glasses," he muttered.

I rounded in front of him and grabbed his shoulders. "Ethan—look at me."

"I think they broke my glasses. I can't find them. *My glasses…*" His voice cracked and his shoulders shook with sobs.

My hand flew to my mouth as my heart split at his distress. Who had hurt him? Was it *Liam*? I gently cupped his face. "Just breathe, okay? Calm down and breathe." Nodding, he exhaled shakily. "Now, who beat you up, Ethan?"

"Zander," he whispered, his breaths quickening. "I have to find my glasses. I can't see a goddamn thing without them." Suddenly, he broke away. "I have to get out of here."

"I can drive you home. You can't see clearly, and you're not thinking straight—let me drive you home."

"No! Just leave me alone!"

Before I could respond, he was off on his bike. All I saw after that was a blur of red. I don't remember storming back up the school steps or demanding to know where Zander was—I just knew that once I discovered his whereabouts, I wouldn't hesitate to confront him, even if it meant entering the boys' locker room. The door slammed shut behind me as I entered.

"Whoa. What the fuck?" someone exclaimed.

"Wrong room, blondie!" came the retort.

"Where is Zander?" I hissed.

A shirtless guy in shorts, with a towel draped over his head, pointed. "He's just getting out of the shower."

Keeping my eyes fixed ahead, I weaved past the half-dressed basketball team until I reached him. There, clad only in a towel with damp skin and hair, Zander stood by his locker with his back turned.

"What the hell is your problem?" I demanded.

He glanced over his shoulder, appraised me, then went back to applying deodorant. I rushed him, shoving him as hard as I could. He stumbled against his gear, sending some items clattering to the floor.

He laughed. "You're one delusional bitch." I slapped him.

"Ah, that was a good one," he remarked. I raised my hand for another hit—but he caught my arm. "Not happening again."

"Why did you do that to Ethan?" I demanded.

He tightened his grip on my wrist, pulling me forward. "Do what?"

I jerked free. "You're an asshole."

He ran his hands through his wet hair, now looking even darker. "You came to the boys' locker room to tell me something I already know?" He shook his head. "I think…I think you came just to see what you're missing out on, right?" He pulled his towel aside just enough to expose himself.

My eyes locked onto his as I gritted my teeth and clenched my fists. "Stay away from Ethan."

"Or what, *Phoebe*?" he challenged.

The sound of him calling me by name sent shivers down my spine. I backed away and ran, not caring who I bumped along the way. I kept running until I reached the restroom, where, finally, that green bean casserole resurfaced.

18

LAURA

"SHE DID WHAT?" I SHOUTED SO FIERCELY THAT A couple of birds scattered from the palm tree above. Mimi and I were relaxing by the pool in my backyard with lime margaritas when Zander called to inform me that Phoebe had grabbed his towel in the locker room.

"I just can't figure her out, babe. She's fixated on me. Everyone saw her giggling and clawing at my towel. She even touched me, L. It was revolting and left me feeling completely exposed. I mean, she knows I'm all yours— I've told her a *million* times."

I gripped the phone so hard I felt like I might break it. Who the hell did that bitch think she was?

"Listen, I gotta run—I'm meeting the coach. I'll call you as soon as we're done, okay?" Then he hung up.

"What, Laura? What happened?" Mimi insisted.

I sank back into the lounge chair, staring at the evening sky—streaked in blue and peach with wispy gray clouds that looked like cotton candy. It turned my stomach. Rolling my eyes, I grumbled at the heavens, "It's Phoebe. Zander says she yanked his towel off in the locker room."

"Why would she even *be* in the boys' locker room?" Mimi asked.

I spun to her. "Who cares? I don't give a damn. She saw him naked, Mimi. I could gouge her eyes out!" I slammed my glass, spilling margarita over the rim.

Mimi leaned forward, a determined glint in her eyes, clearly ready to attack Zander. "Listen, Laura. Zander's a certified piece of shit. Why do you believe any of what he says? He's been ogling Phoebe ever since she moved in— did you forget he dumped you the moment he saw her?

Heat flooded my cheeks as I retorted, "That's so old news, Mimi. Zander's come to his senses. He knows exactly what Phoebe is like, and he's done with her."

"That's what *you're* hoping for, Laura."

"Why else would Phoebe still be after him? It's to hurt

me, obviously. She's madly jealous of me."

Mimi sank onto the lawn chair beside me, her hands resting on my thighs. "Think, L. Phoebe went for the geek. I'm not buying into this Zander fixation. We even knew someone was texting her threats—a secret admirer. To me, that reeks of Zander."

"Since when did you start teaming up with Phoebe? You wanna fuck her, too?"

Mimi recoiled, as if I'd punched her, but I couldn't hold back—she was really pissing me off. After licking her lips and glancing toward the trees, she said, "All I'm saying is, I can smell a rat a mile away."

"The only one stinking up Richmond is Phoebe," I shot back.

Mimi shifted back in her chair and gestured behind me, "Let's hear Phoebe's side then. Here she comes."

I straightened in my seat, my heart pounding. Did Phoebe really have the guts to confront me after what she'd done, or does she think I'm clueless? What a backstabbing *bitch*.

As Phoebe strode toward the pool, I wavered on how to approach her. "Phoebe, want a chair? Margarita?" *With a shot of cyanide?* I raised my glass in exaggerated bitchy mode and sized her up. She looked like shit—splotchy face, bloodshot eyes. Fake crying? She was one hell of an actress.

"No. But could you please tell your boyfriend to back off?" she replied.

I took a measured sip. "Mmm. So good." I clicked my tongue and refocused on her. "I'm sorry, what are you on about?"

"Zander beat up Ethan. And I know it was because I turned him down," she declared.

A jet of margarita splashed from my lips. "Are you insane?" My voice shot up. "What makes you think everything revolves around you?"

"I never asked for Zander's obsession. I did nothing to him. He's just a twisted, repulsive creep. You deserve so much better than—"

"Don't you dare tell me what I deserve!" I exploded, leaping up and invading her space. Mimi promptly stood, her hand gripping my arm, as I fumed, "You think I don't notice your tricks? You're trying to turn me against Zander so you can claim him all for yourself, you sneaky little bitch."

Phoebe, chest heaving, stepped forward slightly. "If he

lays a finger on Ethan again, I'm having my stepdad arrest him."

"Get. The. Hell. Out," I commanded, pointing back the way she'd come. "Now, bitch!" Phoebe glared for a few seconds before retreating. Once she was gone, I wriggled free of Mimi's hold and let out a shriek. I was *furious*—I wanted to choke the life out of her. Just who did she think she was? I shrieked again in disgust.

Mimi gently guided me back to my seat, murmuring, "I knew it," as she shook her head.

"Knew *what*?" I snapped, glaring at her. If I had lasers for eyes, I'd have cut her head off.

"Zander made it up," she explained.

"Don't tell me you swallowed that bullshit—it's just her scheme to turn me against Zander."

"Dammit, Laura. You're too blinded by that asshole. He isn't right for you—no one is," Mimi sighed, intertwining her fingers with mine. "I love you, L," she added, caressing my face with the back of her hand.

I despised her perfume—it was so overwhelmingly sweet, it could give me a toothache. Still, I took her hand and kissed her knuckles. "Do you—love me?"

She pressed my hand against her chest. "With all my

heart."

I paused, nibbling my lip as I feigned deep thought, and gripped her hands tightly. "I was so stupid, obsessing over Zander, that I didn't see what was right in front of me."

Mimi straightened, her eyes glossy, as if I were about to propose marriage. I rolled my eyes internally—*what the hell?*

Swallowing my bitterness, I continued, "I'm so sorry, Mimi. I feel like I owe you something—like ditching that trip to Rome and just being here, every minute spent with you." I kissed her knuckles again.

"Do you really mean that?" she asked.

I nodded. "Of course I do. You're my ride-or-die, Mimi."

She played with a lock of my hair. "You know I'll always be there for you, L."

I stifled a laugh that shit was so easy. "So, after we handle Phoebe, let's take down Zander once and for—"

Mimi pulled away. "One last time? You said spray-painting her locker was the last time. Besides, Zander is the one who—"

"Shh," I hushed her, pressing a finger to her lips.

"We'll get them both. Once we deal with Phoebe, we'll take down Zander by coming out as a couple." Her head tilted in thought. I nodded firmly. "Everyone will know I love you too, Mimi." I grabbed her face and kissed her deeply, struggling to hide my desperation. Our kiss lingered for a moment before she pulled away.

"You promise we'll come out together as a couple?" she asked.

I kissed her again. "Yes." Mimi tenderly stroked my hair and pulled me into a hug. I hugged her back slowly, knowing it would be a cold day in hell before that actually happened.

pHoeBe

Rory handed me another tissue, his voice laced with uncertainty. "I'm sure Ethan's alright."

Every breath hurt. My chest and ribs felt like they'd been pummeled with a baseball bat. With Ethan's face still swollen, he must be in far worse shape. I'd called him every hour with no response. I couldn't understand why he was ghosting me. Did he blame me for Zander's actions? Was it *my* fault that Zander only targeted Ethan after our kiss in the school hall?

"Ethan was hysterical when he left," I explained to Rory. "What if he had an accident on his bike because he couldn't see without his glasses?" I gasped. "What if he's worse off than we thought?" My eyes widened as I sprang to my feet. Ethan could be on an operating table because of me. I should *never* have let him go in that state. What the hell was I thinking?

"Phoebe, stop pacing," Rory admonished. "That's not going to coax Ethan to call back. The guy probably just needs some alone time. He's not ignoring you to hurt you. But what the hell are you planning to do about Zander? He can't just get away with that shit."

Dejected, I sank onto the edge of my bed. "I warned Laura, and I meant every word. I'm gonna tell Rich about Zander if he doesn't back off." Initially, I hadn't wanted to hurt Laura, but her actions left me no choice. She'd never see Zander for the creep he is. And yet, she turned on me so quickly? In my eyes, they were perfect together. I grabbed my phone and texted Ethan:

> Will u PLEASE say something to me?

Rory loomed over me, reading my text aloud. "Hey!" I

snapped, swatting the phone from his hand. He rolled his eyes. "Look, if Ethan really cares, he wouldn't ghost you. Give him some time—he'll text back." Instantly, my shoulders relaxed. Damn, I despised it when Rory was right.

That night, I tossed and turned in a hazy blur of faces—Laura's furious scowl, Zander's idiotic smirk, Liam's weary eyes. Finally, fed up, I kicked off the covers, sat up, and clamped my hand over my mouth to stifle a scream that nearly woke the entire neighborhood. Ethan was at the window, ready to tap, but then he raised a finger to his lips. I jumped from bed and rushed to let him in.

"I didn't mean to scare you," he whispered breathlessly once inside. I left the window open, with the lamppost's glow softly illuminating the room. I stepped back and wrapped my arms around myself, overwhelmed. I'd spent all night worrying about him, and now he was here—I was speechless, both angry and relieved at once.

He slipped his hands into his pockets, nervously eyeing me through a pair of distinctive, oversized round glasses that hugged his cheekbones. The swelling on his face had diminished, though his eye was still a sordid black. Apparently, he was alright after all.

I averted my eyes from him as he began, "Um... I'm sorry for how I reacted. I just..."

"Ethan, you have no idea how worried I was. Why did you ignore me like that?" I demanded.

"I felt embarrassed," he admitted, moving to the edge of my desk and rubbing his hair. "I hated that you had to see me like this. I was scared you'd think the worst, like what my dad used to think..." He pressed his lips together to mask his trembling.

I softened. "Ethan..." I sighed deeply. "I would never think that. I truly care about you."

"Even though I look like that dog with the spot over its eye?" he joked, making me laugh as he stepped into my embrace. "I'm sorry," he murmured against my neck.

"I know you had a tough day," I reassured him, pulling back for a closer look. "Some people even believe Liam killed Miss G because of what happened with your mom."

At that, his face paled and his body tensed. He blinked at me, his Adam's apple bobbing. "Phoebe—my mom didn't kill my dad. I did."

19

pHoeBe

WE STOOD THERE IN SILENCE A BEAT. A SINGLE TEAR slipped down Ethan's cheek as he sniffled and brushed it away. "I understand if—" his words trembled, struggling to form fully. "—your view of me has changed."

Slowly, I lowered myself onto the edge of my bed, feeling winded once again—just like the night Rich told me that Dad had committed suicide. It was déjà vu, complete with the deceit. Ethan had lied to me, and I glared at him. "I think you need to leave."

His head drooped in shame. "I'm sorry," he whispered before climbing out the window.

The next morning, each ring of my alarm sent a surge of throbbing pain through my head. As I finally rose, I caught sight of Ethan's painting, and his shocking revelation flooded back: the sorrow on his face as he confessed—a confession of *murder*.

There was so much about the Littles I didn't know, yet I had fallen for Ethan so quickly. If he had killed his dad, then why was his mom in jail? And what did Liam know about it all?

"Phoebe—are you up?" Mom rapped at the door.

School was the furthest place I wanted to be that day. I couldn't face anyone—Ethan, Laura, Zander, or even Liam's replacement. The idea of them all tightened my chest with anxiety, but I knew Mom would insist on knowing why I lacked the will to go. She'd immediately jump on the phone with Dr. Landry, likely unearthing the sedatives hidden in my laundry basket.

"Phoebe?" she called again.

"Coming, Mom." I inhaled deeply and didn't exhale until I was standing. Whatever awaited me that day, I was determined to face it head-on.

Ethan never showed up at school. I wasn't sure whether I felt relieved or devastated by the absence of his familiar seat in every class we shared.

I hadn't seen Zander or Laura either—until lunch. I sank into a secluded corner seat by the window, away from the crowded, rowdy students. They were serving chicken tacos that smelled delicious, but I had no appetite.

Cradling my face in one hand while idly checking my phone with the other, I found myself hoping for a text from Ethan—or maybe feeling the urge to text him first. Did that make me a terrible person for wrestling with my conflicted emotions about a murderer?

Either way, there was no message from Ethan, only a text from an unknown number. My eyes immediately darted to the back of Zander's head. If he had sent it, he would have already shot me a vindictive look, waiting for my reply. Instead, he was busy chatting animatedly with another basketball player, his laughter boisterous.

I paused, thumb hovering over the message, torn between deleting it or opening it later. Then the room erupted in surprised gasps and giggles; some kids even stole furtive glances my way.

What now? I shifted uncomfortably, knowing it had to do with that mysterious text. Before I could change my mind, I opened it. A series of photos appeared: a girl in underwear, her back turned to the camera, in what appeared to be the locker room.

She looked familiar, wearing a purple silk ribbon in her hair. My hand flew to my mouth. It was Summer—unaware that someone was invading her privacy. But who had taken these pictures, and why send them to me?

I immediately began deleting the photos one by one. It was the very last image that made my stomach churn: Summer's face was partially visible, but someone had doctored pig ears and a snout onto it, captioned with "OINK! OINK!"

A guy at the table in front of me laughed and snorted like a pig. My head snapped up, realizing everyone must have received those same awful images. Who would do something so cruel to sweet Summer? And had she also received them?

An hour later, I found Summer after being summoned to Principal McGee's office, where Mrs. White sat alongside Mom.

"Mom?" I stuttered. "What's going on?" In that moment, memories of the day Dad died flooded back—the faces surrounding me, closing in as I ended up lying on the principal's floor.

"Take a seat, Phoebe," Principal McGee ordered, cutting off my spiraling thoughts. His lips pressed into a thin line as he exhaled sharply through his nose, while Mrs. White stood by with her arms folded tightly.

Those pictures of Summer had clearly infuriated them. But why were Mom and I being called in? I exchanged a glance with her—she returned it with a confused frown and a shrug.

As Principal McGee began explaining, Summer exploded. "I thought you were my friend, Phoebe. How could you do that to me?" She flipped her phone around to display the image with the pig edits.

She couldn't possibly think I'd taken those photos. I blinked, shifting my gaze from her phone to her face. "Wait a minute. Somebody texted me those pictures too. Why are you assuming I did it?"

Principal McGee scowled. "Those photos were sent to nearly every student in this school from a social media account registered in your name," he stated, pointing directly at me.

I felt my face heat up as I dug my nails into my palms. Calmly, I turned to Principal McGee and Mrs. White.

"You need to talk to Laura about this. She's made a fake account in my name before, so I know she's responsible for this as well."

Principal McGee and Mrs. White exchanged a brief look. "Laura told us you would say that," Principal McGee revealed.

"What?" I snapped. "I didn't do it. Summer, please believe me." I turned to her, but Principal McGee and Mrs. White regarded me with skepticism.

"I don't trust you at all, Phoebe," Summer choked out between sobs. Suddenly, she sprang to her feet and staggered out the door. I stood frozen, mouth agape, then looked to Mom.

"These kinds of incidents didn't happen at Richmond, Phoebe—until you enrolled," Principal McGee remarked.

Mom placed a reassuring hand on mine. "My daughter says she didn't do it. So, I assume you will investigate this matter further, right?" I longed to smile or at least show my gratitude that she believed me, but my body felt numb. Did Principal McGee think I was guilty because of previous scandals?

"Considering Phoebe's recent actions—" he began.

"*That was Laura too*. I recorded the video, but I never posted it online. My God, she did that to Summer just to get back at me over a stupid boy—who even sent *me* threatening texts."

Mom turned toward me. "Who threatened you?"

"Do you still have the texts?" Principal McGee interjected.

Damn it, I didn't. My shoulders slumped as I shook my head. "I deleted them."

"Who sent them?" he demanded.

"Zander Bridges."

"But Zander is a model student," Mrs. White objected.

"So is Phoebe," Mom snapped back. "If that boy sent threatening texts to my daughter, I expect action."

Principal McGee nodded. "We'll speak to Zander *and* Laura," he said, glancing at me. "But in the meantime, we can't have you on the cheer and volleyball teams, Phoebe."

"Or PLC," Mrs. White added.

I slid to the edge of my chair and gripped its arms tightly. "Why not?"

"Someone invaded Summer's privacy," Principal McGee explained. "Until we can confirm you're not responsible, we have to impose disciplinary action."

"But—" I squeaked.

Mom squeezed my hand. "Don't worry, Phoebe. It's only temporary. The truth will come out."

My chest sank in defeat. There was no way in hell I would beat the queen and king of Richmond High.

20

MIMI

STRAIGHTENING THE FRONT OF MY POUF DRESS, I took one last look in the mirror to confirm that everything was perfectly in place. The dress was chartreuse—Laura's favorite color. It stopped just above my knees, zipped up at the back, and featured a pleated skirt with a textured design.

I swept my hair into a bun, remembering how Laura always complained that it got in the way during our make-out sessions.

Make-out sessions.

I exhaled sharply and smiled. Never in a million years did I imagine something like this could happen between us. Or better yet, I never thought Laura would ever have feelings for me too.

We hadn't come out as an item yet. But at least with Phoebe off the squad and no longer a Pink Lady, I didn't have to chase after her anymore. I wasn't sure if I was just getting sentimental over Laura, but I felt guilty as hell as I snapped pictures of Summer undressing. Laura had promised she'd make it up to Summer somehow, so I guess we'd have to wait and see.

I blushed as I heard Laura's Porsche honk from the driveway. We were heading to dinner—our official first date.

I spun on my heel, grabbed my purse, and hurried toward the stairs. "I'm going, Nana," I called towards the kitchen. As I opened the front door, my grandma stepped out.

"Wait a second. Let me have a look."

"*Nana*." I quickly eased the door closed so she wouldn't see the car parked out front. "There." I turned in a full circle so she could take in my dress.

"My God, you look as lovely as a graceful rose!" She clasped both hands to her mouth in awe. "Who's the lucky girl?"

My mouth went as dry as sandpaper. "Uh, you don't know her. She's a new member of the Pink Ladies." Internally, I cringed—wasn't I describing *Phoebe*?

"Oh. So, she'll be good to you?" Nana asked, moving toward the door.

I blocked her. "Yep."

"Well, aren't you going to introduce us?"

"We're running late, Nana. I'll see you lat—" My words choked as she nudged me away from the door.

"Why is Lisa's car out there?" she squinted and quickly turned to me. "Are you lying to me?"

"It's *Laura*, Nana, and *no*, I'm not lying. We're double dating tonight."

Nana slowly shook her head. "Baby, that girl is going to hurt you someday."

"Nana, I can't do this right now. See you later." Before she could add another word, I dashed onto the stoop and hurried to Laura's convertible. Normally, I'd kiss Nana goodbye, but her obvious displeasure with Laura irritated me. Besides, they'd eventually have to face the fact that I loved Laura.

"What's with you?" Laura asked once I settled into the passenger seat.

"Just drive," I grumbled, pulling on my seatbelt. Once we were miles from home, I grabbed Laura and kissed the corner of her mouth.

She giggled. "What was that for?" She looked stunning in a maroon pencil skirt and a pink ruffled top. Her hair was pulled back into a ponytail, too. Did that mean a night of passion awaited us?

I settled back with a smile. "Just for being you." I squeezed her knee. "I'm super excited. This is our *first* official date. So, where are we going?"

Laura's dark eyes lit up. "It's a surprise, of course."

I forced a laugh, though a sinking feeling settled in the pit of my stomach. Laura knew I hated surprises.

Before long, we arrived at a restaurant called The Greek Goddess. I'd never been there before, but I knew it was the most popular spot for Mediterranean food. I was just about to gush over how romantic it was when Laura suddenly cried out.

"Look—there goes Zander."

"What?" I whipped around. He waved at us from a table for three in the corner. The floor seemed to tilt beneath me. What the hell was *he* doing here? Was Laura about to break up with him over dinner?

As I struggled to process what was happening, Laura spoke to the hostess.

"We'll sit with our friend over there." She pointed and grabbed my hand. "Come on." If not for her grip, I probably would've stumbled. I glared at the back of her curly head, trying my best to keep it together. "Wow," she murmured as she stopped in front of Zander. He rose to embrace her, kissing her on the lips.

Well, the breakup theory just flew out the window.

Laura glanced at me, her face flushed from being near Zander, as expected. "Let's sit and order."

I slumped back into my seat, arms folded.

"Can you believe Phoebe went to Principal McGee, blaming me for those texts?" Zander asked, clutching Laura's hands across the table. "I don't even know what she's talking about."

"Some asshole did text Phoebe," I said. "She even forwarded a couple of the texts to us." I glared at Zander as he pulled away from Laura, nervously fidgeting with the hair at the back of his neck.

"Do either of you still have them?" he asked. "I mean, maybe if I looked at the number I—"

"I deleted those texts," Laura interjected. "I think she

sent them to herself. Phoebe's such a drama queen. But she has some nerve going to Principal McGee. She accused *me* of snapping pictures of Summer. I would never." She shot me a quick glance and a private smirk. Technically, Laura *hadn't* done that, but she had ordered me to.

"Did you delete the forwarded texts, Mimi?" Zander asked.

No, I hadn't. "Yep," I said, watching the relief wash over him as he assumed he was in the clear. I *knew* that son of a bitch was responsible.

My eyes flicked to Laura, silently checking if she'd caught on, but her gaze was fixed on the menu—which didn't matter since Zander would choose for her. When the waitress approached, sure enough, Zander placed the order.

"We'll have the lamb kabobs over rice with a side of grape leaf rolls."

The waitress jotted that down and glanced at Laura and me. "That all?"

"Yes," Laura chirped, beaming at Zander like he'd got it just right. Laura *hated* red meat.

I slid back in my seat. "Laura, can I talk to you for a

minute? In the ladies' room?" I stood and grabbed her wrist, tugging her along.

She whined all the way to the bathroom. *"Mimi..."*

I shut the door behind us. "What is Zander doing here, Laura? I thought tonight was supposed to be about us."

"Babe—so what he's here?" Her eyes flashed. "Isn't it exciting that he's here and clueless about us being together?" She reached for my hand to pull me closer, but I snatched it away.

"That's not what I want. I can't enjoy my dinner with him sitting right across from me. He sent Phoebe those texts, Laura. He's a fucking creeper."

Laura pressed her lips together and exhaled sharply. "Then that's their business. Phoebe probably pissed him off and he's taking his revenge. Who cares?"

I blinked at her for a moment, then leaned in and kissed her. I needed to know if she felt anything for me. Laura pulled away. "Can we just go try to enjoy our dinner?" She turned and left me standing there.

Nana was right. Laura might as well have stuck her hand inside my chest and ripped out my heart.

21

pHoeBe

"CHARLIE SAMSON CONFESSED AND PLEADED guilty to the murder of his fiancé, Giselle Fischer, last Thursday afternoon," the news anchorman recited for what felt like the umpteenth time that day.

"A week later, and it's still the talk of Richmond Heights," I grumbled.

Rory grabbed the remote and switched channels to his X-Box antics. "But don't you get it?" he asked, bouncing in front of the TV.

"Don't talk like that."

"You only disagree because it was Miss G. If your nerd cheated on you, you'd want to kill him too. Hypothetically, anyway."

My stomach clenched at the mention of Ethan. I hadn't spoken to him in ten days. We rarely crossed paths at school, and when we did, he always avoided me.

"Let me guess—you're still not talking to Ethan?" Rory interrupted.

"You wouldn't understand, Rory."

He paused his game. "Try me."

Even though I knew Mom and Rich were at work, I quickly scanned for anyone else before I shared what Ethan had confessed to me. After I finished, I held my breath and counted to ten—a little exercise I'd started to channel positive energy.

Rory glared silently for a moment before finally saying, "Back it up. The same guy who cried when Zander kicked his ass is suddenly a cold-blooded murderer?" I blinked in confusion. "Phoebe, did it ever occur to you that his father's death might have been self-defense? Heck, I could probably kick Ethan's ass, and you're convinced he's some callous killer."

I wanted to shrink into the couch pillows—I was terribly embarrassed. Ethan must hate me for being so self-centered. All I did was focus on my own feelings when he confessed. I never dug deeper into his story or showed him support. After all, coming forward like that took guts, and he'd trusted me with it.

"I guess I feel for Liam, though," Rory continued. "He lost his job, and he didn't even kill Miss G." He shook his head and went back to his game.

That night, I swung open the door as Ethan climbed up the stoop. "Thanks for coming," I said, stepping aside for him. He kept his eyes fixed on the floor as he passed, trailing me into the living room where I motioned for him to sit.

"So..." I began just as he interrupted,

"I'm sorry."

"No. You don't have to—"

He shook his head. "I need to say this." Leaning against the wall with his arms folded, he continued, "I'm sorry I lied to you. But you're the only person besides my mom who knows."

"You mean, Liam...?" I ventured.

"Not even Liam." His gaze fell blankly for a moment before he added, "My dad choked me unconscious that day."

I gasped. "Ethan, that's awful." I sank onto the sofa

next to him. "You don't have to talk about it if—"

"I want you to know." His eyes searched mine, pain reflected in them. "That day, my dad dragged me to the basement and kicked and stomped me—my chest, my face. I really thought I was going to die. I saw the shovel, and I just..." Tears welled up as he continued, "I didn't mean to kill him, I swear."

"I'm so sorry, Ethan," I whispered, placing a hand on his shoulder.

"Don't be. Not for me, anyway. My mom is the one who deserves sympathy. She's the one who took the blame for marrying a monster, but she shouldn't be locked away. It should be me—" His voice broke.

"No, I'm sure your mom took the blame because you deserved a second chance at life and happiness." I grasped his hand. "I want us to have that second chance. A fresh start."

He stared at me in disbelief. "I expected you'd turn me over to Rich."

"*Why?*"

"Because it's the right thing to do?"

"If that were true, you'd have turned yourself in by now. Why haven't you?"

His head dropped. "Because my mom made me promise not to. I've already broken one of her promises by confiding in you. But you mean that much to me, Phoebe. I trust you with my life." His eyes met mine again—adorable behind those enormous glasses.

I wrapped my arms around him, and he squeezed me tight. I'd missed his embrace so much. As we pulled apart, our faces lingered inches apart. His gaze dropped to my mouth. "Go for it," I whispered.

He cupped my chin and pressed his lips against mine. I tugged him closer, easing my tongue into his mouth as I leaned back against the armrest, drawing him on top of me.

We'd barely gotten started when I heard someone entering through the back door—probably Rory.

"What is it?" Ethan frowned as I suddenly pulled away.

I glanced toward the kitchen. "Someone's in there."

"I didn't hear anything," he replied, leaning in for another kiss.

I grinned. "Of course you didn't." I nudged him off.

"Don't mind me," Rory called from inside the fridge. After a moment, his footsteps thudded up the stairs.

"Anyway, how's Liam doing?" I asked. "I'm sorry about

the mess I caused him—I should've never recorded that video." I gasped, realizing I hadn't told him about everything that had happened lately—Summer's photos and outing Zander to Principal McGee. Taking his hand, I said, "I have *so* much to tell you."

"Well, I'm glad you told someone, Phoebe," Ethan said once I'd finished. "Neither of them should get away with that shit."

"Yeah, but convincing Principal McGee is the hard part. I don't have Zander's texts anymore, and I have zip on Laura."

Ethan toyed with a lock of his hair, deep in thought. After a minute he turned to me. "It might sound cliché, but you could confront Laura with your phone secretly recording in your pocket."

I rolled my eyes. "I think I've done enough recording already."

"True. But that one would be the most important— exposing Laura for who she really is."

I figured I could give it a try. At that point, what did I have to lose?

———

The next day, I waited by Laura's locker, but she didn't

show. Instead, I ran into Summer. She strolled down the hall in a pastel pink blouse with a blue jean skater skirt, her hair neatly tied back with a pink ribbon—she looked stunning.

"Summer—hi."

"Phoebe," she said curtly, her gaze fixed straight ahead.

I noticed a sparkly S brooch adorning her left side. "You're a Pink Lady? Congratulations."

"Yep. And I'm a cheerleader too. They had an opening for both," she replied flatly.

"No one deserved it more than you. I'm really happy for you, Summer."

"Just stop it, Phoebe. Stop pretending to be my friend. I don't need your pity anymore. I've finally succeeded." She started to walk past me, then paused. "I guess I have your stupid prank to thank for that, though." With that, she brushed by.

"Maybe she has a point," said a voice beside me. It was Cassie, arms folded. "Why would you give it all up like that? Did Laura make you do it?"

I took a deep breath. "I didn't do anything, Cass."

She shrugged. "Whatever. I just can't believe Summer got a brooch, and I still haven't."

An idea struck me. I pulled the Best Friend necklace from my pocket. I'd planned to return it to Laura during our confrontation, but seeing how dejected Cassie looked, I handed it over. "Here."

Her eyes lit up. "Really?"

"I don't need it anymore. So, where is Laura?"

"With Mimi in the locker room," Cassie replied, examining the necklace like it was a prized trophy.

That was even better—I could confront them together. There was no way Mimi, Laura's so-called Siamese twin, was clueless.

My heart pounding, I quietly entered the locker room.

"Knock it off, Mimi," Laura snapped. "I said stop." There was some shuffling, then a loud crash against the lockers. I peeked around the corner just in time to see Laura shove Mimi. I held my breath, pressing back against the wall.

"You lying bitch," Mimi seethed, her voice strained, "you never loved me."

Of course Mimi had been in love with Laura. I closed my eyes, wishing I could vanish. Their conversation was intimate and private—none of my business. I'd be damned if I interrupted.

My body tensed as I stepped away from the wall, but then Mimi's words froze me.

"You just used me to do all your dirty work."

"I sure as hell did," Laura retorted.

"What happened to you, Laura? You used to be—"

"Oh, don't even, Mimi. If you knew anything about me, you'd know how much Zander means. You're so goddamn selfish."

Mimi laughed bitterly. "*I'm* selfish? I did everything for you, Laura. *Everything*."

My ears perked up as I wondered if Mimi was referring to taking the pictures of Summer.

"Well, I didn't force you to do any of it," Laura replied.

Mimi took a deep breath. "You're right. But you know what? The walls are closing in on you. Phoebe told Principal McGee about what you did on social media and I have the proof to back her up."

My breath caught and my heart pounded—I needed to hear every word.

"I kept all your texts about setting up Diggs, trying to drop Phoebe at that basketball game, and the pictures of Summer."

Mimi intentionally tripped up at that game? I felt

anger rising so fiercely I covered my mouth with my hand to keep from screaming. I could've *broken my neck*. I wanted to burst in and shake the piss out of Laura, but I couldn't move. I peered around the corner as Mimi continued.

"And guess what? I have forwarded texts from Zander too. That asshole is going down with you."

"Aren't you forgetting that you'll be in just as much trouble?" Laura countered.

"I don't care. I'm done with this shit."

"Babe—you're just upset," Laura pleaded, stepping toward Mimi with arms outstretched for a hug.

But Mimi recoiled. "Fuck off, Laura."

I pressed back against the wall as Mimi stormed out of the locker room, marching right past me.

Shortly thereafter, Principal McGee summoned all of us to his office—Laura, Mimi, Zander, and me. In one breath, Mimi blurted out everything while showing Principal McGee the texts on her phone. Zander sat there stone-faced, glaring at Laura from time to time, while Laura remained silent. Principal McGee saw clear as day that Laura was the instigator.

Straightening in his seat, he declared, "Okay—here's

what I'm going to do. I'm taking this information to the school board, and they will decide what happens next." He shot disappointed glances at both Laura and Zander. "Keep in mind there will be serious consequences. Until then, I suggest you all be on your best behavior."

22

LAURA

"THAT BITCH." I GROWLED, FISTS CLENCHED AT MY sides as I paced by the pool that night. "I can't believe Mimi snitched on me. Not only did she tell McGee, but she did it in front of Phoebe. That damn *bitch*!" I threw an empty wine bottle at the palm tree before me. It bounced off the bark, hit the ground, and rolled into the pool. Zander scoffed from his lawn chair, lounging casually. I glared at him—at his cool, collected demeanor as he lay back in nothing but his boxers.

"What?"

"Why are you losing your shit, babe?" he asked, motioning for me to join him. I stormed over with my arms folded. He sat up and wrapped his arms around my waist. "Remember, both my parents are on the school board. They'll brush this off as a harmless prank." He cupped my chin. "*You* did nothing wrong, and as for that joke about dropping Phoebe—*Mimi* was the one who acted. She just dug her own grave. If you ask me, it was high time you cut ties with her."

A slow smile spread across my face—not because his words comforted me, but because he was trying. But wasn't he right? I hadn't physically done anything; it was all Mimi's fault. Just the thought of her made me cringe— that phony bitch who couldn't have me. Wait a second. I *had* exactly what I wanted. I stared past my boobs to Zander's blond head.

He trailed kisses along my stomach and nibbled the strings of my bikini with his teeth, feigning to loosen them. I giggled, shoving him back against the chair so I could straddle him. Our lips met, and I moaned as his warm hands grazed the small of my back, deepening our kiss. He shifted me against the chair and hovered over me, his hair cascading in a tumble of blond waves around his face.

Mimi should be locked up in a *psych ward* for thinking I'd ever trade this for her.

My legs wrapped around Zander's waist like magnets. He slid his hand to the back of my head and kissed me hungrily.

"Oh, Phoebe," he murmured.

I tore away. "What did you just say?"

"Nothing." He tried to kiss me again but missed as I slid from beneath him.

"You called me *Phoebe*."

"No, I didn't."

"Yes. You. Did." I shoved him hard in the chest. "You're obsessed with her, aren't you?" Had he been fantasizing about her the whole time? Ugh, I was going to be *sick*.

"That was a mistake, babe." He reached for me, but I slapped his hand away like it was filthy.

"Face it, Zander. Phoebe doesn't want you." I burst into laughter until my eyes watered. "She chose a goddamn nerd over you. That's how pathetic you are."

He grabbed my face with a vice-like grip. "Shut the fuck up." His nails dug into my flesh, but all I did was laugh even more. He was that ridiculous—a complete waste. He shoved my head against the chair and then slid off me. "I don't know why I ever took you back. Crazy bitch." He stood up, pulling on his clothes. "I'm *done* with you, Laura."

Only once he was gone did I let angry, salty tears fall. All along, he'd still been hung up on Phoebe. I meant nothing to him. *Nothing.*

Wiping my wet cheeks with the back of my hand, I screamed, "Everybody can rot in hell for all I care—Phoebe, Mimi, Zander, Mom, and Dad. Fuck you all!" I reached for my shirt, but caught sight of someone moving in the corner of my eye. I frowned and pulled the shirt over my head hastily. "What the hell do you want?" I demanded, fussing with my curls, then gasped at the glint of a knife.

23

pHoeBe

everything?" Ethan asked as he sat across from me at the Busy Bean Café that weekend.

"Yes. I feel good, and I'm really grateful to Mimi for doing the right thing. They could've *killed* me with that stunt at the basketball game." I shuddered at the memory. How could Laura pull something like that and then just move on? Did she have no conscience at all? And the way she used Mimi—I couldn't imagine loving someone so much as to do something so awful for them.

"I'm glad, too. I hope they expel Zander," Ethan said,

nervously adjusting his glasses because his eye was still sore. We should've mentioned it to Principal McGee as well, but it didn't matter now—Zander was about to get what he deserved.

My phone buzzed on the table. It was Mom. "Hey, Mom?"

"Phoebe, get home immediately. The detectives need to speak with you again."

I frowned. "About what?"

"It's Laura—she's dead."

Ethan drove me home because I couldn't think straight. How could Laura be dead? I'd just seen her. There had to be some mistake.

I staggered through the front door into the living room, where Mom and Rich were seated with the same two detectives as before—Detective Wren and Detective Santiago.

Santiago stood as I entered. "Hello again, Phoebe. We have a few questions about the last time you saw Laura Preston."

"What happened to Laura?" I demanded.

"You should sit down," Santiago suggested.

"I'm fine. Just tell me."

Santiago glanced nervously at Rich, tugging at the lapel of her steel-gray suit

Rich guided me to the couch. "Come on, Phoebe. Have a seat." Once seated, Rich wrapped his arm around my shoulder, while Ethan lingered in the doorway.

Wren cleared his throat. "Laura's mother found her last night—face down in the family pool."

"My goodness. Did she *drown*?"

Santiago shook her head, her short bob swinging as she exchanged a look with Wren. Why were they being so secretive? Why couldn't they just tell me everything?

Wren turned to me. "Someone cut Laura's throat. Her whole body was covered in slashes—they even split her face wide open."

I clutched my mouth with both hands, silently pleading for Rich to reassure me that this wasn't true. They had to be lying. *Right?*

I gripped my knees, trying to steady myself, and finally managed to ask, "Who did that to her?"

"That's why we're talking to everyone about the last time they saw her," Santiago explained. "We're trying to piece everything together.

"I haven't seen Laura since school—in the principal's

office. Mimi revealed some information about her that would've gotten her into a lot of trouble. But I don't know who would…" Zander? Could he have gotten pissed at Laura? But why? Mimi had the evidence, not Laura. Did she and Mimi have another fight? No way. Mimi loved her—she couldn't have—and yet…who?

"What information are you talking about?" Santiago asked, pulling out a pen and notepad.

I told them everything about what Laura had instigated. But did any of that really matter? Laura was dead—*murdered*. They needed to find her killer, not rehash high school drama.

"So, you could say that Laura didn't like you very much?" Wren asked.

I was at a loss. Laura had pretended to be my friend while sabotaging me behind my back.

"Where were you between eight and eight-thirty last night?" Santiago demanded.

I straightened. There was no way they could believe *I* was involved. "I was at home."

"Can anyone vouch for that?" Wren asked, looking from Mom to Ethan. "We know you were at the precinct," he said, addressing Rich.

Mom shook her head. "I was working late, too."

Ethan and I exchanged a glance. He searched my face for any sign that I wanted him to lie, but I didn't need that. I hadn't done anything wrong. He stepped forward, "Sometimes we study together at eight o'clock."

"Did you study last night?" Santiago pressed.

All eyes were on Ethan, but his gaze met mine. I shook my head—I didn't want him to lie for me.

"No," he finally admitted.

Santiago glanced again at Wren.

"If Phoebe says she was home, then she was," Rich interjected. "Do we need to get our lawyer?"

"Rich!" Mom hissed.

"I can answer their questions. I have nothing to hide," I insisted.

Rich slid to the edge of his seat. "I know you don't, Phoebe. But I'm protecting you."

Santiago dismissed the concern with a wave. "That won't be necessary, Rich. You know how these things go." She forced a smile that Rich didn't return. "As we said, we're just following up with Laura's peers to piece together what happened." Santiago looked me right in the eye. "We *will* catch her killer."

On Monday, Mom insisted I stay home from school, though I really didn't want to. Principal McGee was supposed to announce the school board's decision that day. But would he, given everything that had happened?

I couldn't finish that thought. Laura had done terrible things, but whoever did this to her was a monster.

At school, a shrine had formed at the foot of Laura's locker. Her large yearbook photo hung across the door, and roses, stuffed animals, cards, and candles accumulated in a colorful heap. I felt guilty for not bringing anything. I was lost in thought, admiring the memorial, when Mimi entered. I quickly spun to her. Her usually tidy hair now hung in disheveled strands around her swollen, tear-streaked face.

"I'm so sorry, Mimi."

She glared at me, her eyes filled with fury. "No, you're not."

"Don't say that. Laura and I had our differences—"

"I turned on Laura, and look what happened. I wasn't even there for her..." Her voice broke as she stumbled back against the lockers and slid to the floor, sobbing uncontrollably.

I gently lowered myself beside her. "Laura knew you loved her, Mimi." I reached out to hold her hand, but she jerked it away.

"I don't want your comfort, Phoebe. For all I know, *you* killed Laura.

"*What?*" I flinched and drew back. "How dare you say that? I heard *you* fighting with her in the locker room that day."

Several students gasped and shot accusatory glances at Mimi.

"You bitch!" she roared, slapping me across the face. Then, collapsing to her knees, she lunged over me—grabbing my hair and punching me.

"Stop it, guys! *Stop*!" Cassie cried, trying to pull Mimi away, but Mimi clutched my hair tighter, effectively *dragging* me across the floor by my head.

"Mila, enough!" Principal McGee bellowed as he pushed through the cluster of shouting students. He gripped Mimi's shoulders and lifted her off me. She thrashed, kicked, and screamed curses in my direction.

Through the blur, Mrs. White leaned in. "Let me help you to the nurse's office."

I glanced down at the bloodstains on my shirt. Where

had it come from? I dabbed at my nose and squinted at the red stains on my fingertips. I couldn't even remember her hitting my nose.

"Can you hear me, Phoebe?" Mrs. White asked, waving a hand in front of my eyes.

I coughed, struggling for words. "I'm fine." I slowly rose to my feet, extending my hands to steady myself.

Ethan hooked an arm under me. "Are you alright? What was that about?" he asked, bombarding me with questions while my mind remained foggy. "Your nose is bleeding," he noted gently, cradling my chin.

"I'm alright," I whispered, staring past him at Principal McGee escorting a furious, half-walking, half-fuming Mimi to his office. "I shouldn't have said anything about the locker room."

"She still shouldn't have attacked you, Phoebe."

"Here," Cassie said, handing me a handful of moist paper towels to clean up. I thanked her. "That was weird," she added.

"Yeah. No shit," I muttered.

Later that day, I pleaded with Mom, "Mom, please, I'm okay. We're not pressing charges against Mimi."

Mom huffed in anger, running a gentle hand through my hair. "You should've gone to the hospital, at least. What if you're concussed?"

"*Mom*." I ducked her hand and glanced sheepishly at Ethan, who was sitting on the couch as Mom fussed over me. "It was just a nosebleed."

"How could that girl do that to you?" Mom demanded. "She was supposed to be your friend."

"Mimi is grieving—I get that. But Principal McGee shouldn't have suspended her."

"I'm glad he did something," Mom said as she stood, kissing my forehead. "And that other boy—the one who texted you?"

I rolled my eyes. "Zander. He's suspended too, for a week."

"Is that it?" Mom snapped at me. I couldn't believe it.

"I think they took pity on him because Laura was his girlfriend," I explained.

Mom shook her head. "Rich and I are going to talk to Principal McGee again. That isn't fair at all."

I grabbed Mom's hand. "Will you go to work already?

I'll be fine tonight. Ethan's around until Rich gets back. We're just studying a bit."

She sighed. "Okay, but if you need anything—anything at all—call me. I mean it."

"I will, Mom."

"Okay, see you later." She waved and left.

I moved over and plopped beside Ethan. "I want to call Mimi and check if she's okay."

He tilted his head. "Are you sure that's a good idea?"

"It's the right thing to do. She's hurting. Laura was more than just Mimi's best friend—Mimi was in love with her. I can't imagine what she's going through."

He slid his hand gently along my back. "I know, but I don't think you should call her, considering what happened. She even accused you of murdering Laura. That wasn't fair."

Why would Mimi say that? How could anyone think I was capable of something so gruesome?

"Mimi knew what a bully Laura could be. Their antics almost ruined you, and even with Laura dead, Mimi's still linking you to that mess. You really should have let me be your alibi when the detectives asked."

I shifted to the edge of the couch, moving closer to

him. "Lying would make it seem like I have something to hide. Do you really think I had something to do with Laura's death?"

"Of course not. But this is the second time suspicions have been raised about you."

That was true. The detectives were just doing their job. But what about Mimi? Was she casting doubt on me to hide her own guilt?

I rubbed my temples as a headache started to form. "I can't think about it anymore. Let's put this aside and try to study—at least, focus on something else for a moment." I rummaged through my backpack for my biology book and, at the bottom, spotted something glinting.

Was that what I thought it was?

I squinted at the object—a silver blade with a wooden handle stained with dry blood—a knife.

24

pHoeBe

I CLUTCHED MY BAG, STARING INSIDE IT FOR WHAT felt like an eternity. What on earth was a bloody knife doing in my backpack? I slowly turned to Ethan and said in a low, hushed voice, "There's a knife in my bag—with *blood* on it." I tilted the bag toward him.

Ethan pushed his glasses off his nose and peered inside. "I can't see it," he observed. I reached into the bag to grab it when Ethan suddenly cried out, "Whoa, wait. *Wait*. Don't put your fingerprints on it."

"I can't just leave it there. How did it get into my backpack in the first place?"

"Just dump it in the garbage."

"It's got blood on it, Ethan. I have to take it to the police." I tore a sheet of paper from my notebook and used it to lift the knife. The blade was long and thin, reminiscent of the carving knife from our kitchen set—except this wasn't one of ours. I'd never seen it before.

Ethan stepped into view. "Phoebe—just throw it away."

"*No*. Why do you keep trying to cover for me as if I'm guilty of something?"

"You have no alibi. Mimi accused you in front of everyone. And then there's a bloody knife in your bag that you're about to present to the police and claim you don't know where it came from? There's no way those detectives will buy that."

"But that's the truth. I'm not hiding anything because I *didn't* kill Laura."

———

"Just stay calm," Rich whispered as Detective Santiago approached. Rich and our lawyer, Joan Howard, accompanied me to the precinct after I told them I'd found the knife. Rich carefully sealed the evidence in a sandwich bag to prevent contamination, and he sent Ethan home. Ethan didn't want to leave, but it was for the best—there was nothing he could do to help.

"What brings you all here?" Santiago asked, stopping before us with a coffee mug in hand.

Rich nudged me to explain.

I cleared my throat. "I found this in my backpack," I said, holding up the clear bag.

"That's a knife," Santiago observed, motioning for someone to take it as she pulled up a seat. She grabbed a pen and pad. "Do you have any idea how it got there?"

I shook my head. "None whatsoever."

"As you can see," Joan added, "my client is here willingly, trying to be cooperative and as helpful as possible."

Santiago nodded, tapping her pen thoughtfully. "We're going to run DNA tests on that knife. If it tests positive for Laura's blood, Phoebe, you're in deep trouble. Now, is there anything you'd like to tell me before that happens?"

"Don't answer that," Joan interrupted.

"But I don't know anything!" I snapped at Joan. "If it is Laura's blood, then the real killer planted it in my bag to frame me."

"Stop talking, Phoebe," Joan said. "We brought you

the knife. Even if the victim's blood is on it, you can test for prints and show that they don't belong to my client. Let's go, guys."

I looked to Santiago for a comeback, but she said nothing. Slowly rising to my feet, I tried to think of something else that might prove my innocence. "Laura made a lot of enemies. The suspect list shouldn't stop with me."

Laura's funeral was a week later, and it was a total disaster. Mrs. Preston threw a fit when Mr. Preston arrived with a young blonde on his arm. The three of them cursed and screamed at each other so ferociously that the church members had to remove them, and the entire ceremony was delayed for nearly half an hour.

Laura's casket was closed, but Mimi wouldn't leave until she'd seen her friend one last time. When the clergy finally relented, Mimi lost it—insisting that the body wasn't really Laura's. She wouldn't stop screaming about the stitching down the center of her bloated face.

I couldn't bear to look. I wanted to remember Laura as she had been alive—the beautiful, feisty, headstrong girl you either loved or despised.

The reality was, she would never be either of those again.

MIMI

I shoved the bottle into my backpack and tugged on my jacket. It was Wednesday, well after midnight. I hadn't slept a wink since Laura's death. Every night since her funeral, I'd visited her grave to talk to her. I needed her to know how sorry I was. I never meant for things to happen the way they did. I wouldn't stop going to the cemetery until I was *convinced* she'd forgiven me.

So, I quietly slipped out of my room again.

"Where are you going?" Bianca demanded as she stood in the doorway of her bedroom, her sparkly Hello Kitty lamp glowing behind her.

"Why are you awake?"

She folded her arms. "I heard you shuffling around all night." Her eyes fell on the bag I had shifted to my other arm. "Are you running away?"

I started toward the staircase. "Go back to bed."

"I'm gonna tell Papa."

Shrugging, I continued towards the stairs.

People always talked about how spooky the cemetery was, but even at night—with the full moon hidden behind clouds—it wasn't frightening at all. Perhaps I'd just gotten used to it, since it was now Laura's resting place.

I pictured the olive quilt on Laura's queen-sized bed—the same bed on which I'd once made out with her.

And yet, Laura made it clear that'd meant nothing.

I stopped in front of the tombstone where she lay six feet beneath me. My lip trembled as my fingertips traced the engraving: LAURA JEANETTE PRESTON, GONE BUT NEVER FORGOTTEN

I clutched the tombstone with both hands, my tears falling onto the damp dirt.

Laura was never coming back. And we hadn't even been on speaking terms when she died. I had promised her I'd always be there, and I'd thrown her to the wolves.

I crumpled to my knees, struggling to breathe. "I'm so, so sorry, L. I didn't mean for any of that to happen. I just wanted us to be together." A low, sickening moan escaped my lips as I hung my head and sobbed.

I sniffled and wiped my cheek with the back of my hand. "I brought us a drink tonight. It's your favorite—

vodka."

I remembered when we first tasted vodka—when we were fourteen at Laura's parents' anniversary party. They wouldn't let us have any champagne, so Laura said we'd have to settle for water. Instead, she emptied the water bottles and filled them with vodka. We were bold enough to drink it in front of everyone.

Laughing bitterly, I pulled the tall vodka bottle from my backpack, tilted my head back, and took a long, messy sip. The clear liquid ran down the sides of my face.

"I knew I loved you that day, L. I loved your humor and your wit. You were fearless—always going after what you wanted. You inspired me to be who I am—proud and unapologetically gay." The trees rustled in the wind, and a shiver crept up my spine. My shoulders huddled closer as I pulled further into my jacket. I knew I should probably head back home, but I wasn't ready to leave yet. I couldn't accept that Laura was in that grave. How was I supposed to move on?

I let out another devastating sob and accidentally let the vodka bottle slip from my grip. It hit the dirt with a thud, spilling its remaining contents. I knelt, gripping handfuls of moist soil.

"You weren't supposed to die, Laura," I whispered, my eyelids fluttering before widening in alert. Someone was coming. Sniffling, I straightened and turned just in time to see a figure pick up the vodka bottle and raise it high above their head.

25

pHoeBe

"I WANT TO CANCEL MY APPOINTMENT FOR TODAY," I told Dr. Landry's secretary just before lunch on Wednesday.

"Sure. Would you like to reschedule?"

"Uh, can I just call back after I've checked my calendar?" I replied.

"Of course. I'll let Dr. Landry know you can't make it. Anything else I can do for you?"

"Nope." I hung up, already determined not to book another appointment. Seeing Dr. Landry wasn't helping my credibility anyway. Santiago and Wren had dropped by yesterday again to discuss the school board situation;

they still hadn't received the lab results from that knife, and I still didn't know how it ended up there.

I slipped my cell back into my pocket and headed for the cafeteria when Cassie rushed up, shoving me so forcefully that I slammed against the lockers.

"Are you going to come after me next? Because we can settle this right now," she said, stopping just inches from my face.

I stared into her angry, red-rimmed eyes. "What's your problem?"

Her face twisted with sorrow. "The cops found Mimi."

My heart pounded. "What do you mean the cops found Mimi? Was she missing?"

Cassie shook her head amid sobs. "She's *dead*."

My hand flew to my mouth. "How? Wait—why the hell are you accusing me? I know nothing about what's happening!" I didn't even realize I was screaming and shaking.

"Then why are you always at the police station?" Zander interjected, popping up beside me—his suspension over already.

"The detectives are questioning me because of the shit you did," I snapped, jabbing a finger his way. "I'm pretty sure they're grilling you just as much since Mimi's the one who had evidence that you're a creep."

Cassie folded her arms and glared at Zander. "So, it's true? You were Phoebe's creepy admirer?"

Zander scoffed. "You girls really need to get over yourselves. Besides, Phoebe—the cops didn't find a bloody knife in *my* book bag." He turned his nose up at me before walking away.

Cassie dropped her arms. She, Summer, and a couple of other cheerleaders eyed me suspiciously. "What's he talking about?"

"It didn't happen like that," I insisted.

Summer gasped. "So, they did find a knife, Phoebe?"

"No—*I* found a knife in my backpack and took it to the police because it wasn't mine. Somebody's setting me up, and I think it's *Zander*!" I yelled in the direction he'd gone. I mean, why else would he know about the knife unless he had planted it?

"Laura said you were jealous of her, Phoebe," Summer added, peeking at me as if she were afraid to look. She wrapped her arms around herself and stepped away. "But I didn't think it would go that far."

"Right—which of us is next, Phoebe?" Cassie asked,

disgust dripping from her voice.

My lips trembled, but I refused to cry. I was tired of the constant accusations. I spun around, shoving past the crowd of students who had gathered, and collided with Principal McGee.

"Phoebe, just the person I was looking for. There are two detectives here to see you."

I let out an exasperated breath as Santiago and Wren came into view.

Mom, Rich, and Joan joined me at the precinct a short while later while the detectives questioned me about Mimi's death. They explained they'd found her body on top of Laura's grave—someone had smashed her face repeatedly against the tombstone, knocking out most of her teeth.

I had never heard anything so gruesome. I needed a paper bag to stop hyperventilating.

"Can't you see you're upsetting her?" Mom asked Santiago.

"We need to know when she last saw Mila, that's all," Wren offered gently.

But how could he speak so calmly, with those

disturbing details etched in his memory? Mimi had died *horribly*.

"Students say you and Mimi fought the other day. What was that about?" Santiago pressed.

I blinked my wet lashes and shook my head, unable to speak.

Mom wrapped an arm around my shoulders, pulling me close. "Mimi attacked Phoebe. My daughter never laid a finger on her."

"Then why did Mimi go after you, Phoebe?" Santiago asked impatiently.

I licked my dry lips, struggling to remember. I couldn't move past Mimi's murder. I couldn't understand why we were playing *20 Questions* instead of patrolling the streets for a killer. I glared at Santiago through teary eyes. "You need to get whoever did this to her."

Joan reached over to Rich and gripped my knee. "Tell them what you know, Phoebe. Explain what happened during your fight with Mimi."

"Laura's death hurt Mimi—a best friend and lover would feel that way. That's what happened."

"So, why turn on you?" Santiago asked.

I glanced at Joan, who nodded encouragingly.

"Because she believed I murdered Laura. Once gossip starts, it never stops. People think I'm some twisted murderer just because you keep questioning me. I didn't do anything to anyone. And why aren't you talking to Zander? His creep meter has gone off more times than I can count."

Wren cleared his throat. "Well, we've spoken to Zander and his family, and his parents can confirm he was at a behavioral retreat following the school board's decision. He wasn't even in Richmond Heights when Mimi died."

Joan leaned forward. "Phoebe has answered all of your questions as best she can."

"And I wasn't the only one in conflict with those girls," I added. "They fired teachers because of Laura and Mimi—Liam Little and Mr. Diggs too."

"So while you're busy questioning Phoebe, her life could be in danger too, if someone's targeting teenage girls," Rich stated, making the air drain from me once again. I hadn't once considered that I might be the next victim.

"We've spoken to both Mr. Little and Mr. Diggs," Santiago said. "They have solid alibis. Where were *you*

Wednesday, around midnight?" she demanded, locking eyes with me.

"Midnight?" I squinted in disbelief. "I was home—in bed—asleep."

"Phoebe's curfew is at eleven," Mom pointed out.

Santiago looked from Mom to Rich. "But can anyone confirm she was home?" Neither answered.

"That means nothing," Joan said. "And if you don't have any more questions, we'll be leaving. Come on, guys." We all stood up.

"Well, there is something," Wren interjected, halting us. "You'll be happy to know that the knife tested negative for human DNA."

"Human DNA?" Joan repeated.

"Yes. It turns out it was fish blood," added Santiago.

"None of it makes sense," I murmured later that night. I rolled onto my stomach to face Rory, who sat at my desk, running his hands through my fuzzy journal from Miss G. "Leave that alone."

He threw up his hands. "I'm going to read it anyway once they arrest you."

"Haha, Rory, the comedian."

He mimed an air drum roll and hissed a symbol. "Seriously though, Phoebe, if those idiot cops think you're capable of murder, they need to reconsider their career choices."

"The killer planted that knife in my bag to make me look suspicious. I want to believe it was Zander because he knew about the knife, but then again, he could have learned about it from his sister, Officer Bridges."

Rory scrunched his nose. "But why fish blood?"

"Because someone has a twisted sense of humor." It hurt my brain to sift through the facts. Nothing was clear except that someone wanted me blamed for the murders—those horrific murders. I couldn't stand to think about it, as it felt like a wound reopening on my body.

"Wait a second." I pulled myself upright and crossed my legs. "The texts. Oh my God. *It's Zander*." I covered my mouth with my hands.

"What are you talking about?"

"Remember the Valentine poems? He threatened to kill me—to slash my torso, kick out all thirty-two of my teeth. That's exactly what happened to them, Rory."

"True. Except the knife doesn't fit."

"Zander placed that knife in my bag, thinking I'd hide it. He never expected I'd take it to the police. He still thinks he scares me."

Rory rose and began pacing. "Okay, say it isn't Zander. Who else can be tied to that knife?"

I chewed on my bottom lip. Fish blood... "Somebody gutted a fish and then planted that knife in my bag?" I gasped, and suddenly we both started crying in unison—

"*Summer*."

All Summer ever talked about was fishing. Sure enough, that knife could be hers. She had every reason to hurt Laura and Mimi too, once we found out they had taken those pictures of her. I frowned. "But then, why frame me for it? I did nothing to Summer."

Rory stopped in front of Ethan's rose painting. "He went on that fishing trip too."

I gulped, my heartbeat quickening. "You think Ethan killed them because…?"

"They hurt you. You got kicked off the squad and everything else." He shrugged.

"Again, why pin it on me?"

"Maybe because he spilled his secret to you. I don't know—I'm grasping at straws here." Shaking my head, I grabbed my cell. "What are you doing?" Rory asked.

"I'm going to get to the bottom of this. Ethan and Summer are the only two who would have a knife smeared with fish blood. One of them must have slipped it into my bag to frame me. I need to know who—and why." I texted Ethan Summer's address, asking him to meet me there.

pHoeBe's mom

"Phoebe—" I rapped at her door and pressed my ear to the wood. Silence greeted me on the other side, yet I never heard her leave. I knocked once more. "Honey, I'm coming in." I cautiously entered. Phoebe wasn't there. I glanced at my watch: 11:22.

Why would she be out past curfew with a murderer on the loose? Or maybe she was with Ethan—either way, she should've told me where she was going.

Sighing, I shook my head at the laundry basket by the door, clothes draped over its rim. Maybe I'd put them in the machine for her. I lifted the basket, and something rattled inside. Frowning, I emptied its contents onto her bed; a pill bottle fell out.

"What's this?" I whispered, holding it up to my eyes. It was a sedative that had been prescribed to Phoebe a few weeks ago. I unscrewed the cap and poured all fifteen pills into my palm. She hadn't taken a *single* pill.

Phoebe had told me that Dr. Landry thought she was fine, and I *believed* her. With everything going on, of course she'd need a sedative eventually. How could I have been so oblivious to this—and for how long?

"How long have you needed medication?" I muttered, my eyes scanning the room as if it might reveal an answer. They landed on a teal, fuzzy book on Phoebe's desk. It looked like a diary, but it wasn't locked. Without a second thought, I flipped to an entry from a few days ago. I skimmed several lines, and suddenly the floor seemed to drop from beneath me. The journal slipped from my trembling fingertips as I stumbled away, fumbling in my pocket for my cell phone.

God, no. Not again.

Finally, my shaking fingers managed to dial Rich, who answered on the first ring. "Rich! Come home now. Phoebe's doing it again."

26

pHoeBe

"LOOKS CREEPY," RORY WHISPERED, FOLLOWED BY a pitiful ghost impersonation.

I rolled my eyes and shut off the engine. "Will you knock it off? This is serious." I peered out the passenger window at Summer's house—it looked eerie in the dark, and all its former southern charm had vanished. Perhaps that was a sign.

"So, what's the plan?" Rory asked.

I gripped the steering wheel and shrugged, unsure of what to do. "Well, I'm just gonna come right out and accuse them both," I said after a beat. "I'll let my phone record everything in my pocket. Somebody is bound to slip up, and we'll outnumber the culprit."

"Hmm. But what if Ethan and Summer are working together?"

"I hope not. If they are, we'll have our work cut out for us."

Rory snickered. "Sounds like a stupid plan."

I bumped shoulders with him. "Then you should do just perfect. Let's go." I climbed out of the car and slouched up to the stoop where the front door was slightly ajar. "Hello?" I called, waiting for a response. Glancing at Rory, I shrugged and stepped inside. "It's me, Phoebe. Anyone home?"

Their dimly lit living room was furnished with old-fashioned, seventies-era pieces. I turned into the hallway toward the staircase when muffled sounds from the kitchen made me pause. I held my breath, straining to hear—a bump followed by a cough.

I barged into the kitchen. "Summer, I need to talk to…" I froze, staring at Summer sprawled on her back, choking on her blood.

Dropping to her side, I called out, "Summer!" Her eyes met mine as her blood-soaked hands clawed desperately at the air. A deep slash marred her throat. "Oh my God,

Summer." I whipped out my phone to dial 9-1-1, but someone swatted it from my hand. It clattered across the linoleum and slid under a counter. I spun around, startled. "*Cassie?*"

Clutching a bloody knife and grinning devilishly, she said, "Surprise! I wasn't expecting you so soon."

I blinked in disbelief as she stared back—her eyes wild, hair matted to her damp forehead, with a smear of blood on her cheek.

"Cassie, what the hell are you doing? Give me your phone."

She stood before me, tapping her foot. "No."

"Are you crazy? We have to help Summer!" When she didn't budge, I dropped onto my stomach and scrambled beneath the counter for my cell.

Cassie lunged, grabbing my ankle. I thrashed free, kicking her aside. My fingertips brushed the phone. I stretched my arm and slid it toward me. Still lying on my stomach, I began dialing for help—when a sharp pain stabbed my left calf as the phone hit the floor again. I screamed, rolling onto my back and drawing my knee to my chest. Cassie had *stabbed* me.

"Look what you made me do," she hissed.

"Fuck!" I shut my eyes, wincing as warm blood streamed down my leg. Clutching my knee, I moaned, "Cassie, why are you doing this?"

"Is the Queen Bee seriously asking me that?" She hovered over me and pressed the knife's tip to my neck. "I should cut your throat even deeper than that bitch's." She glared toward Summer with furious eyes. "It all goes back to you, Phoebe. *You're* the reason I killed Laura and Mimi." Then she pricked my cheek with the knife.

Do something, Phoebe! My brain screamed, but my body remained paralyzed. Where the hell had Rory gone—to get help?

"Those bitches were so obsessed with you there was no room for Trailer-Trash Cassie." Her eyes brimmed with emotion, though no tears fell. She pressed the tip of the knife beneath my chin. "You robbed me of a scholarship that night at the Wild Cats game."

"What? Cassie, I didn't—" There was no point in finishing that sentence. Assigning blame was useless. Laura was dead. And Cassie had killed her.

"I'm sorry, Cassie. I had no idea." I tried to sound sincere, keeping my voice steady.

"Of course you didn't. You were so wrapped up in your

little perfect world, with all the boys vying for your attention." She smoothed a hand through my hair and giggled, "I gotta thank you for sharing Zander's poems. I wouldn't have gotten so creative with my murders if not for that."

How could she casually converse while we bled out on the floor? My throat tightened as I glanced at Summer, lying a few feet away, unconscious—I prayed she wasn't dead.

Cassie followed my gaze and then turned back to me with a bitter smile. "Summer and I went on a fishing trip too. I knew you'd suspect Summer after finding fish blood on that knife." Her eyes flashed. "I even thought of pinning it all on Summer after Laura gave her a brooch. You know I still never got one? *I* was a Pink Lady before you and Summer. But did they deem me worthy? Nope. I worked my ass off on the squad. I deserved that scholarship… for baby Joey…" she whispered, a tear dropping from her lash, then turned away for a moment, sniffing.

She had to let me call an ambulance. Summer needed help immediately.

"Cassie, look at me. It's not too late for you." I

grimaced at the throbbing in my calf, fighting back tears. I gritted my teeth, forcing a steady tone. "I promise we can sort everything out after we call for help. Don't make this worse for you. Think of your family—your mom and baby brother."

She shot me an accusing look, her voice cracking, "Joey's not my brother. He's my son." She trembled with sobs. "I tried to do everything right. I needed that scholarship, but you dumb bitches got in the way with your stupid, *stupid* games!" She raised the knife to stab me. I screamed, grabbing her hands and struggling to pry the blade from her grip. She broke free and stabbed the linoleum near my head.

I glanced toward the doorway, expecting Rory to appear—where was he? "*Rory*! Rory, *help* me!"

"Who the hell is Rory?" Cassie grunted while pulling the blade free.

What did she mean? She knew Rory—he had a crush on her, on all the cheerleaders. I froze, confused, even as Ethan appeared behind her and wrestled her away.

"The police will be here any second now," Ethan said, keeping a tight hold on Cassie with her arms pinned behind her back.

"Where's Rory?" I repeated, staggering to my feet. My left side throbbed as I hobbled toward Ethan, panic swelling in my chest. "My brother—*where is he?*"

Ethan slowly shook his head. "Phoebe, you don't have a brother."

Yes, I did! I brushed past him, stumbling through the house, searching everywhere, calling for Rory—begging him to come back. But he didn't answer.

27

pHoeBe

IT HAD BEEN THREE WEEKS SINCE CASSIE'S ARREST, and they admitted me into the mental health facility. Dr. Landry described Rory as a reincarnation of Dad for me—Rory was his middle name. I began imagining Rory in the hospital as I recovered from my suicide attempt. He became my guardian angel, filling the emptiness when I was alone, making me laugh when I was sad, and talking sense into me when I was confused. He made everything better. I knew that if I took Dr. Landry's prescriptions again, my happiness with Rory would vanish. But what I hadn't realized was that it was all in my head. The support I had relied on from Rory was really my own decision—I comforted myself during my worst times.

"Right this way," the nurse said, gesturing toward the visitor's lobby. I peeked through the glass window and saw Ethan seated at a table in the back. I exhaled a shaky breath before strolling over to greet him, relieved that my leg had healed with no serious damage. I walked with a limp at first as I underwent physical therapy, but after a couple of weeks, my calf was fine.

Ethan stood as I approached, flashing that adorable crooked grin. "Hi," he said.

I reached out to hold his hand, but he pulled me into a tight embrace. I relaxed in his arms, glad he was there. "Hi," I echoed.

"Are they treating you okay?"

I rolled my eyes. "Well, they're not exactly laying out the red carpet." He chuckled, pushing his glasses off his nose. I spotted a paper bag standing beside his feet. "What's that?"

He pulled out a sketch pad and handed it to me. "I know they don't allow sharp objects in here, so I sketched some stuff and left blank pages for you to finish when you leave."

I flipped to the first page—a sketch of a girl sitting on a crescent moon. It was beautiful. I closed the book, deciding to explore it later. "That was sweet of you, Ethan."

His eyes darted around the lobby at the other patients gathered with their loved ones, engaged in hushed conversations. He shoved his hands inside his pockets. "Hey, I saw Summer today."

"Summer," I repeated, feeling a sense of warmth wash over me. Things were looking up for her. Thankfully, she was recovering quickly. Had Cassie cut even an inch deeper, she could've severed an artery. Summer had lost quite a bit of blood and needed a transfusion, but overall, she was okay. I even heard Mrs. White had selected Summer as the new president of PLC *and* captain of the squad.

"Summer says she looks forward to you being her co-captain," Ethan said, slipping his hand inside mine and wrapping his other arm around my waist. His big eyes studied my face behind his glasses. "Are you okay?"

"You mean, do I still see Rory?" I asked. His lips parted in hesitation. "No. I don't see him anymore. I've let Rory go," I said proudly. Finally, I could let Dad rest in peace.

GO GRAB YOUR FREE BOOKS

When you subscribe to my mailing list, you'll instantly get *The Perfect Daughter* and *The Perfect Ride*. Plus, you'll be the first to know about my new releases, special offers, and other fun stuff. (Rest assured, I will *not* flood your inbox. ☺) Visit nikikeith.com to get your download.

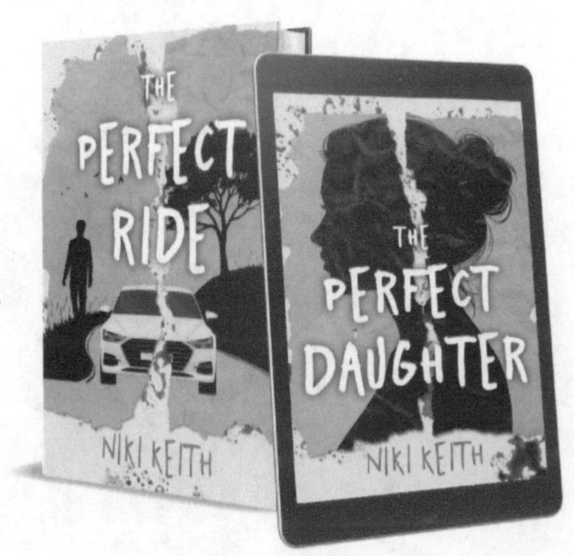

I'D LOVE TO KNOW YOUR THOUGHTS.

Reviews mean everything to an author. I would be really grateful if you could share your honest opinion about *Crush* (it can be as short as you like.) And if you *did* enjoy *Crush*, be sure to check out **nikikeith.com** for what's coming next.

I can't thank you enough for giving my book a chance. Take care! ☺

ABOUT THE AUTHOR

Niki Keith writes twisty young adult thrillers about broken teens doing wrong things for all the right reasons. These days she prefers tea over coffee, dreams of going outer space, and is still searching for the best rice crispy recipe.

When she isn't murdering fictional characters, she's cuddling with her affectionate love-biting kitty, pondering what to read next from her TBR pile.

You can connect with Niki on her website nikikeith.com.